Justice for Crockett

Corby Taggart has always walked in the shadow of his favoured elder brother, Link. Eventually the seething rivalry between the two siblings was bound to boil over, but nobody in the New Mexico town of Cimmaron could have predicted the violent results that would ensue.

Forced to flee to prevent an untimely audience with the hangman, Corby takes to the owlhoot trail under the handle of Kid Silvers. Link's pursuit of his wayward kin leads him into the wild, yet beautiful high country of Wyoming's Yellowstone Valley. There he encounters an old hunter by the name of Beartooth Crockett who exerts a powerful influence on him.

So when the old guy is brutally slain, Link is determined to bring the perpetrators to justice. The final showdown with the Silvers gang will prove whether blood is indeed thicker than water.

Justice for Crockett

Dale Graham

A Black Horse Western

ROBERT HALE · LONDON

Robert Hale Limited
Clerkenwell House
Clerkenwell Green
London EC1R 0HT

Typeset by
Derek Doyle & Associates, Shaw Heath
Printed and bound in Great Britain by
Antony Rowe Limited, Wiltshire

ONE

LOST

Link Taggart shrugged deeper into the warmth of his sheepskin jacket. Even though it was the hottest time of year, a numbing chill ate into his bones. The golden orb blazing down from a deep azure firmament had lost much of its intensity. This was not surprising as he had climbed more than 6,000 feet up into the heartland of Wyoming's Rocky Mountain fastness.

For the last six days since leaving Thermopolis, he had not encountered another living soul. Sure there had been signs, and all of the redskin variety. But they had kept their distance, for which he had been more than grateful.

He shivered involuntarily. And it was not merely due to a sudden gust of cold wind attempting to tip him out of the saddle. Link was becoming increasingly concerned, worried even.

His meagre supplies were exhausted. And for a man used to having a general store within easy reach, the bleak wilderness stretching out to the distant horizon was not something to lighten the burden that pressed hard onto his broad shoulders. Especially since he hadn't eaten in over twenty-four hours. Even then, it had only been the unappetizing gnaw on his last stick of beef jerky. Hunger pangs gripped his stomach with a vengeance. And taunting images of a two-inch rib-eye steak smothered in thick gravy didn't help.

He drew the chestnut mare to a halt. Another search of his saddle-bags revealed nothing more than a half-chewed apple. It was brown and shrivelled, but a swig of water helped it slip down his gullet, pips and all.

Surveying the awesome rigour of the valley below, Link couldn't help but marvel at the stoic grandeur of the landscape. Harsh mountain peaks soared high on either flank. Their rugged sweep, etched starkly against the brilliant blue of the sky, contrasted with the sombre darkness of the endless marching ranks of pine forest. And scurrying along the valley bottom, a silver thread pursuing a serpentine course eventually disappeared amidst the savagely eloquent battlements of serried peaks. Was it any wonder that man had seen fit to bypass this rugged landscape in his search for new lands to settle?

Link shook his head in bemused astonishment.

To a man raised on a cattle ranch, the sight was overwhelming and inspirational, yet at the same time infinitely terrifying.

But it was too late for turning back now. He had burnt his bridges, so to speak. And his quest was nowhere near complete. In fact, it had barely started.

All he knew for certain was that he was somewhere in the Absaroka Range. But just exactly where, he hadn't the foggiest notion. An old army scout boasting the lyrical sobriquet of 'Stinkweed' Dawson on account of the potent aroma that exuded from his person had told him to keep a weather-eye open for the Sugar Loaf.

'Cain't miss it, young feller,' he had spouted volubly after imbibing more than a few slugs of 'red label' hooch, courtesy of a somewhat naïve Link Taggart. He had come across the old guy in the Evening Star, one of the innumerable drinking-parlours in Thermopolis. Or, more likely, it had been Stinkweed who had latched onto an easy source of free booze. Greenhorns were always fair game to frontiersmen.

'Easy to find as that, is it?' posed Link, wide-eyed and innocent.

Stinkweed had nodded earnestly whilst filling his glass.

'Sure thing, mister,' he burbled. 'Looks just like a birthday-cake topped with icing. Keep it on yer right side and yer won't go wrong.' Stinkweed had belched loudly, much to the hilarity of other drinkers. The old-stager had ignored their mocking disdain, rising unsteadily to his feet.

'You sure it's as easy as that?' reiterated a rather sceptical Link Taggart.

'You doubtin' the word of Stinkweed Dawson?' the old miner responded with a pained grimace, as if it was inconceivable that he could be mistaken. 'Figure I'm only after bummin' a free drink?'

'Of course not,' Link hastily assured his bleary-eyed companion. 'I just don't want to get myself lost out there. That's all.'

'Didn't I just tell yuh?' warbled the old-timer, repeating the standard response to all his directions. 'Yuh cain't miss it. Once over Togwotee Pass, it's all downhill to Moose Jaw.

Be there inside of a week.' Another lurid belch, then he staggered off in search of his pit to sleep it off before accosting the next sucker.

So far Link had not set eyes on the elusive Sugar Loaf. He had begun to figure that it only existed in the soused imaginings of Stinkweed Dawson. He also recalled the old soak mentioning a gap in the mountains known as Togwotee Pass, slap bang on what was known as the continental divide. Everything to the west poured into the Pacific Ocean, the rivers on this side filling up the Missouri and all points south. According to Stinkweed, there was a signboard announcing this important fact to the world.

Link cast a jaundiced eye over what he desperately hoped was the bleak rock-girt notch of Togwotee.

Nothing.

Shoulders hunched disconsolately against the keening wind, he jigged his mount forward, allowing the cayuse to pick her own way through the tightly packed phalanx of upright conifers. The trail he had been following had faded to a narrow deer-run which had finally petered out two days before. All he could do now was keep heading west, trusting that the good Lord would see him right.

Within minutes, the dense swathe of trees had closed in around horse and rider. He was effectively cocooned in a sombre twilight world that exuded an unworldly, almost surreal, atmosphere of gloom. In all his twenty-six years, Link had never experienced such a deep sense of isolation.

Total and inexorable, it was unnerving in the extreme.

He was certainly no milksop, and could hold his own in any bar-room fracas with the roughest of hard-assed rannigans. But this was different. He was up against the forces of nature in the raw, and felt out of his depth, unable to cope with the rigours of survival in such a harsh and unforgiving environment.

He ought never to have been taken in by a devious old jigger like Stinkweed Dawson. Leaving Thermopolis without a guide had been a big mistake. He had been warned, and offers had been made. But Link Taggart knew best. A tough guy of his ilk didn't need a guide to lead him by the nose.

The realization that such offers were proposed with a serious intent had come too late.

And now he was lost.

'At least I've still gotten you, Smudger,' he murmured into the chestnut's right ear. The horse gave a brief nod, baring her jutting canines in a companionable grin.

But there was no denying the truth of the matter. And the thought of being cast adrift in this vast wilderness gave him no comfort. With another cold night in the open fast approaching and no hot food in his belly, Link was rapidly losing heart.

Another two hours went by with no indication that the impenetrable curtain of trees was ever going to part. The sombre interior of the forest had slowly but inexorably surrendered to night.

Link plodded onward, head bowed on his chest as the aching paroxysms of hunger tightened their rancid grip on his innards. He had not laid eyes on so much as a single rabbit that could have provided a meal.

Then he saw it.

Only by chance had some instinctive sensation told him to look up. He shook his head to clear the cobwebs from his lethargic brain. It was still there, about one hundred yards ahead. Only faint, but a glow all the same, warm and inviting.

But was it friend or enemy?

Indians? Shoshone or Blackfeet maybe, who would just as soon peg out this hated white invader of their tribal lands as look at him.

Link was almost past caring. All the same, his natural instinct for survival advised caution.

Stepping down off the faithful Smudger, he stroked the chestnut's muzzle, whispering soporific endearments. Then he carefully drew the .36 Whitney revolver from its oiled holster and checked the loading. Silently he moved through the intervening screen, taking advantage of any bushes to conceal his approach to the mysterious light.

An orange flicker materialized. It appeared to be a small camp-fire, but he could hear no sound of voices. Maybe it was a lone traveller like himself. Never had Link been so eager to encounter his fellow man.

As he emerged into a small, open glade, his uneasy gaze panned the surrounding shadows, trying to pick up on any alien presence. The fire hissed and crackled but the clearing was empty. Link's starved senses latched onto the mouth-watering aroma of meat roasting on a spit. To a half-starved itinerant, the delicious scent was overpowering.

He gave one last look round, then he lurched over to the fire and snatched up the sizzling carcass of a rabbit. Eyes watering with fevered anticipation, he raised the tempting repast to his open mouth. But he never got the chance to sample the tasty treat. A gruff voice, deep and resonant, lanced through the darkness from behind.

'Keep yer hands where I can see 'em, stranger.' The blunt injunction was uttered in a firm, yet tight drawl. 'And drop that there hogleg nice and easy-like.'

Brown eyes bulging, Link froze – rigid as a stick of beef jerky.

'You shuck that smokepole now, mister,' repeated the voice. The snarled order, low yet menacing, was supported by the long barrel of a Hawken rifle. 'Else I'll plug yuh here an' now. Then eat yer carcass meself.'

'There was nobody here,' Link croaked rather feebly whilst quickly discarding the revolver. 'And I haven't eaten in a coon's age.'

'That's no excuse for bustin' into a man's camp and stealin' his victuals.' The guttural rasp had hardened. 'In these parts, that would be reason enough for doin' away with the thief.' A sharp click from the cocking rifle brought beads of sweat bubbling on Link's anxious brow.

'No need for that, mister,' he said quickly, holding his arms out all the straighter. 'I can pay for the food. Pay you double if that's what you want.'

His captor grunted.

'Anyone else with yuh?'

'No!' replied Link. 'Just me and Smudger.'

'Eh?'

'The chestnut mare. Called her that after the white splashes on her nose.' Gaining a little confidence now that he knew this dude was a white man, and not about to gun him down immediately, Link lowered his arms and made to turn around.

The Hawken jabbed into Link's side.

'Keep them mitts where I can see 'em,' hissed the man tersely. 'Might be easier all round if I was to plug yuh

11

straight off.' He chuckled gleefully. The rasping clamour emerged more like a throaty cough. 'Ain't decided yet.'

The man leaned across and retrieved the rabbit from Link's hand. There followed a series of grinding and crunching noises. It sounded like a pig in heaven and was followed by a satisfied belch of approval.

'Cooked to perfection,' announced the hidden camper. 'You can turn around now so's I can see what sort of thievin' critter was after robbin' me of my supper.'

Link slowly spun on his heel, both hands still raised.

Facing him, Hawken long rifle cradled in one hand, a half-chewed rabbit in the other, stood a giant of a man. Long black hair cascaded from beneath a wide-brimmed leather hat bedecked with interlinked bear claws and sporting a large eagle-feather. Link considered himself a well-built jigger at six feet, but this man mountain towered over him by a good six inches. He was clad from head to toe in fringed buckskin ornamented with beads and porcupine quills. A rough straggly beard dribbling with rabbit-juice encompassed a set of hard, grey eyes. Their flinty gleam appeared to be probing deep inside the intruder's very soul.

The big man tore another chunk of meat from the skewered rabbit as he carefully assessed his captive. One eye seemed to have a permanent squint, a feature occasioned by the livid scar that ran from his left ear down to the corner of his mouth.

Neither spoke for a full minute. Link figured him to be around the middle forties mark. Although it was difficult to judge the guy's age with any degree of accuracy beneath all that hair.

'Where's yer pack-mule then?' grunted the bearded man.

'I'm only carrying what's in my saddle-bags,' replied Link feeling rather sorry for himself 'And that's only a change of clothes and some tobacco.'

The hunter scoffed at this remark.

'Mean to say yuh trekked into the mountains with no proper supplies?'

'Old feller down in Thermopolis told me to look out for the Sugar Loaf. Said I couldn't miss it. But I haven't seen hide nor hair of the goddamned thing.'

'Where was you makin' fer?'

'Moose Jaw.'

The trapper raised a jaundiced eye.

'And does this Good Samaritan be havin' hisself a name?' enquired the big man charily.

'Indian scout called Dawson.'

'Stinkweed?' howled the other, shaking his big head with uncontrolled mirth. 'That old scrope still bummin' free drinks?' He didn't wait for a reply. 'He couldn't give proper directions to the end of the street.'

At this point the big man's face relaxed. He threw the half-eaten rabbit across to Link who caught it and immediately set to work. Table manners taught by his mother were forgotten as pure hunger took over.

Five minutes later, only the bare bones remained, picked clean with every shred of meat devoured.

'Man, you sure weren't kiddin'.' The hunter whistled, handing over some sourdough biscuits. These too I want the same way.

'Told you I was lost and hadn't eaten for nigh on two days.'

The hunter replied with a tight guffaw, then added as an afterthought, 'The Sugar Loaf is some forty miles north of here. You're way off course.'

Link's jaw dropped. 'So where am I?' he asked, gratefully accepting a proffered mug of steaming coffee.

'This here's a side valley off the Yellowstone,' announced his benefactor proudly. 'Nobody lives here, 'ceptin' me, of course – Jubal T. Crockett, otherwise known as Beartooth.' A platelike hand gently fondled the string of canines that encircled his neck. 'I've done named it Beartooth Valley. My cabin's at the far end, a full day's ride from here.' Crockett smiled, a wistful expression softening the rugged contours of his weathered visage.

'Link Taggart,' announced his guest with evident relief and holding out a hand. 'Pleased to make your acquaintance, Mr Crockett.'

The mountain man took the extended hand and squeezed. Link's eyes popped as the vicelike grip threatened to crush his fingers into dust. He knew this was a test, some kind of frontier game. How he played it would depend on Crockett's continued goodwill. Holding the other man's narrowed gaze, he held his breath, keeping a straight face, blank and inscrutable. Eventually Crockett relaxed his grip, nodding with approval.

'Folks generally call me Beartooth,' he said releasing the mangled appendage. 'Exceptin' on Sundays, of course.'

'Sure am glad I ran into you, Mister ... erm ... Beartooth.'

'Glad to have your company ... *Mister* Taggart,' purred the mountain man with a sly grin. 'Don't get many visitors in this neck of the woods – especially those what have gotten themselves lost.' He shook his big head, a serious cast clouding his dour features. 'Easy as fallin' off a log fer

14

a tenderfoot to lose his way in this country and just disappear.'

'That thought had crossed my mind,' agreed Link.

Crockett paused long enough to haul out a sack of tobacco. He extracted two clay pipes from his pocket and stuffed them with the black weed. 'You'd have made a nice tasty supper for some mean old grizzly,' he opined, lighting them both. Handing one to Link, the trapper smiled to himself as the younger man cautiously eyed the smouldering bowl. 'Don't bear thinkin' on, do it now?' Then he chuckled loudly as the pun struck home. 'Don't *bear* thinkin' on. Good one, eh?' Crockett's broad shoulders shook with glee.

Link couldn't help but join in. Then he sucked hard on the clay pipe stem. The result was a violent paroxysm of coughing.

'Never smoked a pipe before?' enquired Crockett, offering a crafty smirk.

Link shook his head, unable to voice any response. His face had turned a vivid puce.

'Shouldn't oughta inhale this stuff,' continued his companion, stifling a fit of laughter. 'Could rightly do yerself a serious mischief.' He puffed away nonchalantly on his own pipe, casually rolling the smoke round his mouth before allowing it to dribble from the corner of his mouth.

'Thanks all the same, Beartooth,' muttered Link after recovering his equanimity. 'But I figure it's safer sticking to normal stogies.'

Crockett shrugged. 'Suit yerself.'

For some minutes, the two unlikely companions smoked in silence, each swathed in his own thoughts – not to mention smoke.

An owl hooted in the distance. Occasionally, they heard the faint scuffling of some woodland creature stalking its prey. Otherwise, a total sense of peace and tranquillity enfolded the small clearing.

It was Link who broke the relaxed ambience. An inquisitive expression played across his handsome features.

'Forgive me butting in, but I've been wondering,' he said.

'Yeah?'

'Where did the handle of Beartooth come from?'

A booming laugh broke from the big man's open mouth.

'Me talkin' about grizzlies spooked yuh, then?'

'Just curious, is all.' Link's shoulder lifted as a spiral of blue smoke filtered from between pursed lips.

Crockett's eyes narrowed to hard chips of coal, black and intense as he cast his mind back in time. Slowly the years rolled away as a wistful expression softened the hard leathery features.

TWO

GRIZZLY ENCOUNTER

'It all began some three years back, after I'd fmished scoutin' for the wagon trains.' Crockett's gruff vocals lowered to almost a whisper as reminiscences jostled for position. 'Fancied a change of scene. A new beginning. I'd done a heap of trappin' in my early years. That is until the beaver stock ran dry.' He poked idly at the fire with a stick. 'Too many hunters all after a piece of the action. We bled the high valleys of all there was. Then the fashions changed. Silk came in and beaver-hats were no longer the thing to be seen wearin'.'

Crockett went on to outline how he'd missed the life; the challenge of pitting his wits against the elements, living off the land, having no one to answer to but himself. And so he had taken off, heading back to the high country of the Grand Tetons he loved so much.

But things had not gone according to plan. Only five days out of Thermopolis, he had been taken prisoner by the Blackfeet. Crockett was forced to watch a fellow captive being disembowelled and his entrails eaten by the tribe. But his own stoic resilience under torture won him the respect of the tribal chief. Yellow Hand had then challenged him to a foot race.

The prize was to be his own life.

Stripped naked, he was given one hour's start. The race lasted five days. He had managed to kill three of his pursuers before eventually eluding the others. Thanks in no small measure to his ability to live off the land, he survived, ending up here in Beartooth Valley. And the Blackfeet had never bothered him since.

Indeed, such was the respect and esteem in which this courageous white-eye was held that Yellow Hand had offered his sister to Crockett as a bride. She was a beautiful girl and the trapper had been more than happy to accept such a generous gift.

The soliloquy suddenly dried up.

Crockett's broad shoulders slumped. His whole being seemed to wilt.

Eventually he regained his composure and continued.

It seemed that the woman had died the previous spring. Tears welled in the trapper's eyes at the recollection. It hurt, hurt bad. He had loved her dearly. Now once again he was on his own. Gnarled fingers strayed to the string of yellowed teeth around his neck.

Link noticed the furtive move but said nothing.

'So what kept you in the valley?' he enquired, now thoroughly enthralled by the story.

'Game!' exclaimed Crockett with a twirled flourish of his moustache. 'And plenty of it. Nobody had trapped here before, so there was fox, rabbit and deer for the takin'. And not only that.' His eyes gleamed in the fire-light. 'At the last rendezvous I attended down at Jackson I found out that beaver were back on the menu. Seems like them natty hats is back in fashion. And this valley is chock-full of the little varmints.'

'So what about the Beartooth moniker?' pressed Link.

'Just comin' to that,' admonished Crockett, taking a long swig of moonshine.

The trapper had not stopped talking for a full hour. Perhaps it was down to the solitary existence, being out here all on your own for months at a time, surmised Link. Before resuming his monologue, the mountain man stood and heaped a couple more logs onto the fire.

'Best to keep it goin' all night,' he responded to Link's questioning look. 'Keeps any hungry critters at bay. The ones to watch out fer are the wolf-packs. Then there's them damn grizzlies.' His jaw tightened as he peered deep into the glowing embers of the fire. 'Yeah!' he repeated in a hoarse whisper edged with suppressed loathing. 'Them fellers ain't afeared of anythin' – animal or human.'

Then it all came out.

Slowly and remorselessly. As if it had to be dragged from his very being. The gunmetal eyes shrank to tiny pinpricks glinting in the flickering light. The thin lips drew back, tight as a drum.

'Me and White Dove, that's my wife.' Beartooth offered his hands to the heat of the fire. 'Prettiest little girl this side of the Sierras.' A pensive aura of melancholy then clouded his seamed face before he continued, 'We was out hunting for deer to stock up the larder. She'd wandered off to collect berries, nuts and suchlike, whilst I settled down with the Hawken.'

Crockett paused to relight his pipe, chewing hard on the thin stem. His breath came in short bursts and he struggled to maintain control as the macabre scene rushed back to haunt him, flooding his mind with dark, wretched images.

Link laid a hand on the trapper's shoulder.

'You don't have to tell me if the memory is too painful,' he said quietly.

Crockett shook his head, squaring his shoulders.

'About time I got it off my chest. Bin festerin' too darned long,' he replied, trying to inject a note of gruffness into his cracking voice. It didn't do for a mountain man to show too much emotion, especially in front of a stranger.

A coyote howled in the distance. The wind sighed in the surrounding trees reminding Link that nights in the mountains could be exceedingly cold. He shivered, tugging the saddle blanket round his shoulders.

Crockett resumed his tale of woe.

'I had the deer in my sights, finger on the trigger. And all set to haul off. That's when I heard it.' He stopped, eyes staring blankly at the fire.

'Yeah?' urged Link.

'A stomach-wrenching growl followed by that scream.' Crockett shook his big head, then hurried on. 'It was like no other sound I ever heard. A crazed howl of pure terror. I knew straight away she'd been attacked by a grizzly.' The trapper lumbered to his feet, pacing up and down the clearing as if to gear himself up for the final purge of his conscience. And like a foaming cataract in full spate, the words flooded out. Unstoppable and forthright.

'It was only a matter of one hundred yards to the point

20

where I'd left White Dove,' he said. 'Nothin' really, but it seemed like ten miles. . . .'

Covering the rough ground at a frantic pace, Crockett had ignored the thorny saplings that whipped at his exposed face. The bear's incensed snarl grew increasingly louder, more terrifying. Such was his panic that he failed to notice that his wife's deperate screams were fading.

Drawn by the animalistic baying, he finally burst through a screen of dwarf willow into a scene from hell itself. Unmoving, White Dove lay at the feet of the towering black beast. And it was monster, at least seven feet tall. Its bared teeth and claws were dripping red. Crouching on one knee, Crockett just pointed the rifle and fired.

The bear had staggered back a pace, hit in the shoulder. But the lead shot appeared to have little if any effect on the lumbering beast.

It turned to face this new enemy. Teeth gnashing furiously, it reared up to its full height. Then charged – straight at the intruder. There was no time to reload. Grasping the rifle by its barrel, Crockett had swung the weapon over his shoulder, and waited.

When challenged, bears can move at a fearsome pace. And this one was no exception.

Twenty yards, ten, five.

Crockett tensed. He had to get this just right.

The beast's deadly incisors had filled his vision, snapping voraciously.

The heavy rifle swung, catching the charging animal high up on its snout. Such was the intensity of the blunt strike that the weapon flew out of Crockett's hands. The bear shuddered under the hard impact. It howled in fury, forelegs waving frantically.

21

Yet still it came on, the lethal claws reaching out.

Whipping out his hunting knife, Crockett had stepped to one side and lunged at the creature's exposed belly. He felt the razor-sharp blade bite through the tough hide. Slicing upwards, he had the satisfaction of seeing the bear's own life-force gushing forth. An ugly smile, devoid of all feeling, had cracked the trapper's hard exterior.

But the grizzly was well-named. It was not finished yet. Critically disabled, it was still capable of inflicting severe injury. With one final swing, the creature's left forepaw twisted, raking this human invader with its lethal claws.

Crockett had yelled as the sharp nails tore at his face. He staggered back out of range from further injury. Like an exposed rib the bone handle of his knife poked from the creature's black and red belly. The bear had tried to come after him, eager to finish its brutal task. But time had run out. It tottered. A choking gurgle escaped from the open maw as the huge creature keeled over, muscles twitching as its claim to life expired.

Breathing hard, and clutching at the torn flap of skin ripped from his cheek, the trapper reeled drunkenly across to where his wife lay still. Only the briefest of examinations was necessary to inform him that she was dead.

Sinking to his knees, he had clasped her to his chest. Unrestrained tears soaked through the matted tangle of his greasy beard as the painful memories flooded back. And there he remained, wrapped in his grief, until darkness eventually brought him back to reality.

Crockett fingered the necklace encircling his neck. The hard line of his mouth eased. He felt better now that he had been able to tell his story. Removing his hat, he ran a thumb over the linked claws – and smiled.

'I took her back to our cabin and buried her in a shady nook overlooking the valley.' His blank, almost dead eyes slowly widened, the tightness around the mouth relaxing. 'You are the first person I've told that to,' he said. His voice was stronger now, more alive. Jubal Crockett had finally buried his demons.

'I sure feel honoured, Beartooth,' Link vouchsafed, feeling a touch embarrassed. 'Me just stumbling in here like that and sharing your supper.'

'That's the way of the mountains,' commented Crockett, filling up Link's cup from the blackened coffee-pot. 'Share and share alike. A man never knows when he might need help. Just like you did.'

Now that the trapper had opened his mind and his heart to this young fellow, he was becoming more than a mite curious as to why he was out here. Crockett was itching to ask the question. But on the frontier, a man's business was his own affair. You accepted a fellow traveller at face value. Took him as you found him. What he'd got up to in the past counted for nothing. It was how he behaved in the here and now that mattered. If Link Taggert wanted to unburden himself, he would do so in his own good time.

And until then, Jubal T. Crockett would have to rein in his restless curiosity.

To cement this new-found alliance, Beartooth handed back Link's shooting-rig. The younger man nodded, acknowledging the placatory gesture.

'That's a smart-lookin' pistol you've gotten there, Link,' enthused Crockett, narrowing his peepers a smidgen. 'Looks like a piece that's seen some action.'

Link could sense that this mountain of a man was bursting to learn more about the tenderfoot stranger who had stumbled into his solitary existence. The big man was just too civil to ask, didn't want to pry.

'Some,' replied Link with a noncommittal grunt. 'Mostly hunting deer and getting rid of critters on my father's ranch.'

Not one who would normally open up to strangers, Link hung back. He had the feeling that Beartooth Crockett was angling to know if he could face off more than just dumb creatures.

Link stared into the glowing embers of the fire.

In the months since his return to the Box T Ranch at Cimarron in north-east New Mexico, Link had deemed it prudent, essential even, to learn the rudiments associated with the use of firearms. Now that he had graduated from law school in Chicago, he hoped that such knowledge would not be required of a legal attorney. But life in the western territories demanded that a man could at least protect himself. Thus far, he had thankfully not been called upon to use the weapon against any human varmints, of which Cimarron had more than its fair share.

Link cast a surreptitious glance towards the trapper. He was beginning to feel at ease in the company of this primitive frontiersman. Even though their acquaintanceship had been a mere few hours, already he considered he knew the man. Maybe it was the fact that Crockett had saved his bacon, and shared his supper. Not to mention unburdening his most intimate thoughts to a complete stranger.

Perhaps the trapper felt the same bond of understanding, a mutual empathy.

Link sensed the hunter's hawkish eyes likewise appraising him across the dancing tongues of flame. Even if he had wanted to satisfy his benefactor's curiosity, at that moment he was too damned tired to think straight. The warmth of the fire, the welcome food, not to mention the shots of home-brewed moonshine with which Crockett had laced his coffee – all were having a soporific effect on both mind and body.

Link's head drooped. His eyes flickered unsteadily.

'Reckon I ought to be getting some shut-eye,' he mumbled, flipping a spent cigarette-butt into the fire.

'That's a good notion,' responded Crockett. 'We need to be up early if I'm to set you on the right trail for Moose Jaw.'

Link stood up and stretched the stiffness from his weary muscles, then wandered over to his tethered horse.

The mount idly looked up from a succulent tuft of grass. It's OK for you, considered the young man as he removed the heavy saddle and unhooked his bedroll. Animals can always find something to keep them going. Reading his mind, Smudger gave a perceptive nod before turning her attention back to nature's bounteous feast.

Settling down beside the glowing embers, Link wished his *compadre* good-night. Then he closed his eyes, huddling down into the comforting warmth of his blanket. He was just drifting off into a deep sleep, when suddenly. . . .

THREE

UNWELCOME VISITORS

A savage growl pierced Link's addled brain. Was it a dream, a nightmare? He'd only just that minute put his head down, or so he thought. Another growl cut through the dark curtain of night. This time it was closer and over to his right.

'Shift yer ass, boy. Them's wolves come a-callin'.'

The strident warning from Beartooth Crockett instantly brought Link out of his torpid stupor. Shrugging off the trail-weary lethargy of minutes before, he leapt to his feet, grabbing for the holstered six-shooter by his side.

'How many d'you figure there are?' he rapped, unable to hide the nervous twitch in his voice.

'Two for sure,' replied Crockett, peering into the gloom. His thumb stroked the hammer of the loaded Hawken. 'Maybe three. They obviously smelt the rabbit.'

Link grabbed hold of a burning branch from the fire and wafted it towards the screen of pine trees that surrounded the clearing. They said that wild animals were afraid of fire. So why had these creatures come so close?

26

'Are they likely to attack?' he asked.

'Depends how hungry they are.'

Both men were bent low, their bodies tense as bedsprings. Link prayed hard that the wily beasts maintained their distance. It was one thing shooting a harmless deer, quite another defending your very life against known predators.

More savage growls, low and menacing, sent shivers of dread tumbling down Link's spine. The creatures were difficult to pinpoint in the dark. His straining eyes panned the clearing, searching for any sign of movement. Flickers of red seemed to hover in the opaque murkiness of the surrounding forest, then disappear.

'Can you see them?' he asked in a tremulous croak. His mouth was dry, his tongue rough like hard leather. At the same time, globules of sweat erupted on his forehead – the result of fear rather than heat from the firebrand.

Crockett was given no time to reply as a ferocious howl rent the air, louder and more raucous than previously.

He just had time to rap out an urgent warning.

'Here they come!'

But from which direction, he could not tell.

At that precise moment a huge adult male, its mottled fur sleek and glistening in the light cast by the fire, emerged from the screen of pine trees. Without any hesitation, the creature hurled itself across the open clearing. Its teeth were bared and dripping saliva, and the creature's ugly snout wrinkled in a nauseating rictus, as its red eyes focused with burning intensity on the exposed back of Beartooth Crockett.

If the creature had not announced its intention to attack, the trapper would have been doomed. As it was, he whirled in a slick pirouette, the Hawken raised and spit-

27

ting flame. The ball of lead struck the wolf squarely between the close-set eyes. A perfect close-quarter shot. The animal was dead before it hit the ground.

But their leader's battle cry had been the signal for the other members of the hunting-pack to make their presence felt. Two more fully grown beasts bounded from cover. Their thick pads hammered the earth as they charged. One dived at Crockett, knocking him to the ground. He could smell the animal's fetid breath, its exposed fangs gnashing only inches from his face. The single-shot Hawken was now useless.

The trapper's life hung in the balance. All he could see were the smouldering ruby eyes and the snapping jaws working in feverish anticipation of its next meal.

Then –

Two shots rang out. Both from a sidearm. One struck the attacking wolf in the side. The animal yelped in shock from the heavy impact. Badly wounded, its momentum was severely curtailed. Even so, it still had sufficient strength to lash out with its front leg, the jabbing claws raking Crockett's left cheek-bone. Hardly noticing the open wound, the trapper desperately scuttled back, crab-like, out of range.

It was the second blast from the Whitney that finished the job, the slug driving hard through the wolf's skull.

On witnessing the terminal results of the attack on its colleagues, the third member of the pack hesitated, dropping into a furtive crouch.

A stunning silence, thick and heavy following the cacophony of sound, descended on the clearing.

But only momentarily. The remaining wolf was hungry. Like its human adversary, it had not tasted meat for too

28

long. Soundlessly, it rose up, cautiously edging forward at the ready. Then, in a single willowy bound, it dived at Link's exposed flank.

'Watch out!' yelled Crockett. 'On your left!'

Link sensed the looming yet deadly presence out of the corner of his eye. Instinct for survival immediately took over. Throwing himself to one side, he swung and fired. Three times the revolver bucked in his tight fist. Only one bullet hit the target. But that was enough. The wolf uttered a choked squeal of pain; its large head was thrown back as the .36 calibre lead slug struck hard through bone and gristle. Rolling onto its back, legs kicking at the air, it bleated fitfully as life rapidly ebbed away.

Both men were breathing hard, sucking in mouthfuls of blissful oxygen.

Crockett eventually lumbered to his feet. He held out a hand. Link took hold and hauled himself up off the floor.

A look of disquiet creased Link's angular features. Crockett noticed the tight set of the mouth.

'Some'n wrong?' he enquired.

'That wolf sure has left its mark on you.'

The trapper gingerly felt the flap of loose skin hanging open beneath his left eye. He winced as the realization filtered down to his tightly strung nerve-ends.

'Needs stitchin',' was all he said, the words flat and coolly delivered. 'Reckon you've gotten the bottle, mister?'

Link's eyes bulged. Things were happening too fast for him. One minute eating rabbit, the next being attacked by marauding wolves. And now being asked to take on the roll of a frontier sawbones.

He shrugged. 'Just tell me what to do.'

Before commencing the primitive operation, Crockett imbibed a liberal dosage of moonshine. Likewise, his appointed if temporary surgeon felt the need of a hefty belt to calm his own frayed nerves.

Then he set to work with a light-hearted quip, trying to bolster a modicum of confidence he certainly didn't feel.

'This is going to hurt me a sight more than it'll hurt you.'

'You reckon?' came back the blunt retort.

Following Crockett's instructions, Link carefully sewed up the gash using implements from the trapper's medicine-bag. It took thirty minutes and ten stitches. Crockett's grim face remained set, deadpan, throughout what was clearly a painful ordeal. He was one tough character.

Link breathed deep, letting out all the built-up tension. He uttered a short laugh.

'Now both sides of your ugly puss match up.'

'Seems like I'm beholden to you now, Mister Lincoln Taggart.' The trapper grinned.

'Nothing like a man earning his supper,' offered Link, thumbing fresh shells into the revolver. 'Now if we're through preening ourselves in this mutual admiration society, perhaps we could have us a cup of coffee and get some sleep?'

Crockett joined in the easy laughter.

'Don't know about you,' he said, 'but I could sure use a snort of something a mite stronger to send me off into the land of Nod.'

There was one other job that required Crockett's attention before he could allow himself to settle down for the night. He gathered a fresh armful of kindling and set another fire burning brightly on the far side of the clearing. It didn't do to take any chances where wolves were concerned. There might well be other packs in the vicinity. Once he was satisfied that both fires would last the night, he wandered across to his own bedroll.

His gaze took in the huddled figure on the far side of the fire. The tough leathery features softened. Even though the mountain man had spent as much time in the company of nature and the elements as with his fellow man, he figured he was a good judge of character. Knew whether a jasper was playing him false or not. And he had come to the conclusion that Link Taggart was a square guy. On the level. A bit naïve in the ways of the frontier perhaps, but he would soon learn.

The guy could have been the son he and White Dove never had. Deep trenches around his eyes twitched at the notion. Then he heaved another log onto the crackling embers, poking life into the glowing heart of the leaping flames.

Crockett had already been up for a half-hour preparing breakfast when Link eventually surfaced. The wolves had been skinned, their pelts scraped clean. They were even now drying out beside the fire.

'Fancy some wolf-steak with yer beans?' A beaming grin widened on seeing Link's ogling peppers. 'Waste not, want not. That's what I allus say. Yuh can't be too choosy in the mountains, young feller.' Then he added whilst chewing on a sliver of meat: 'A bit stringy perhaps, but us trappers don't often get much chance of sampling wolf. And them pelts will fetch a pretty penny at the next rendezvous in Jackson.'

Link accepted the plate and tentatively prodded the blackened hunk of meat. With avid relish, Crockett tucked into his food. Link followed with a mite less enthusiasm. The trapper peered at him over the rim of the tin plate, stifling a grin.

31

Then he said, 'Mind if I have a look at that handgun of your'n?'

After the previous night's encounter, he had determined to get himself a revolver. He had never previously felt the need of a sidearm. Not that he had any intention of ditching the Hawken. There was no other long gun to match it for accuracy and distance. But he had seen the need for more concentrated firepower when the chips were down. And a revolver would meet that need.

Link nodded, handing over the Whitney.

'It's been rechambered to accommodate cartridge shells,' he offered, mouthing a spoonful of beans. 'My pa swore by the Whitney. He always preferred them to Colt's Navy model.'

'You sure knew how to use it last night and no mistake.' Crocket removed the Whitney from its custom-made holster and read the inscription etched into the polished blue of the octagonal barrel.

To my eldest son, Lincoln, on his 16th birthday. From your loving father.

'That was ten years since,' mused Link. 'A lot of water has flowed down the river since then. But I've always kept it.' His shoulders lifted in a shrug. 'Although it's been stuck in the presentation box for most of that time, until recently.'

Crockett sensed that here was an opportunity to delve a little deeper without it appearing that he was snooping. He cleared his throat, then casually enquired, 'You gotten a young kin then?'

The somewhat blasé nuance injected into the remark was not lost on Link. His mouthed creased slightly as he heard the sardonic direction in which the trapper's thoughts were running.

A younger brother. Corby Taggart had a lot to answer for.

FOUR

THE MALCONTENT

The two Taggart boys had been born four years apart. Both to the same parents, they had also been raised on the same ranch in the Cimarron country of northern New Mexico. But there the similarity ended. In temperament, they were as alike as chalk and cheese.

The elder boy, Lincoln was more comfortable around books, preferring the schoolroom to the open range. From an early age it was clear that, of the two, he had the brains. Rarely did he fail to achieve top grades in class.

Right from the beginning a bright future was mapped out for him. A well-read woman, his mother offered every incentive. Even his father, a cowman born and bred to the open range, couldn't help informing all and sundry that Lincoln was going to make the name of Taggart respected throughout the territory.

Even had he embraced the notion, Corby Taggart realized he could never aspire to such dizzy expectations. As a result, he deliberately courted trouble at every turn. As a cowpoke, Corby was second to none. He could throw a young calf and have it branded faster than any other puncher on the Box T. To him, bookwork was a waste of time. And he resented all the attention that his parents lavished on his elder brother. As time passed, a festering resentment slowly ate away at Corby's soul. Simmering below the surface, it was inevitable that one day it would boil over.

On a Saturday night when Lincoln stayed home reading the works of some obscure dramatist called Shakespeare, Corby was off hell-raising in Cimarron's juicy flesh-pots with the other hands. More than once the town marshal was forced to intervene when the younger Taggart threatened trouble. A night in the cells to cool his heels usually did the trick.

But for how long? That was the question the marshal kept asking himself.

Things might have come to a head had not Lincoln won a scholarship to attend the prestigious University of Chicago. With his elder brother away from the family home for four years, Corby Taggart was able to regain his confidence and keep a tight rein on his petulant temper.

It didn't stop him getting into scrapes with the law and his father having to bail him out of the hoosegow. But Jacob Taggart was well respected as the biggest rancher in the district. Not to mention the wealthiest. His money had helped place Cimarron on the map, raising it from a humble stop-over on the Santa Fe Trail to a thriving centre of commercial endeavour, boasting a schoolhouse, church and hospital.

Jacob had also made certain of his own financial security by establishing a general emporium to service all the needs of the ranching community. From fencing wire to saddle tack, *Taggart's* could provide it.

A few indiscretions from Jacob's younger son could be overlooked – providing nobody was badly hurt. Thus far, Marshal Chuck Holliday had managed to keep the feisty kid from killing anybody. Nonetheless, he knew that sooner or later Corby would let his gun hand do the talking.

All too soon, the four years had passed.

And now Lincoln Taggart was back, having graduated from law school with honours. All that Cimarron required to ensure its future prosperity was a legally qualified attorney. And Jacob had every intention of servicing that need by setting up his elder son in his own business.

Everybody of note from around Colfax County was invited to the sumptuous homecoming party at the Box T. Somehow Corby was able to maintain an unctuous smile on his face. But it took a monumental effort of will power. Had anyone bothered to take a close look at the younger Taggart, they would have noticed the icy glimmer in his dark eyes, a tightness around the weak jaw-line, teeth bared in impotent fury.

Nobody did.

The party went off smoothly.

But the die was cast. It was now only a matter of when, and how the malcontent would react. For react he surely would. Four years in the position of top dog was not about to be easily relinquished.

'What yuh gonna do, Corby?'

The hesitant query broke from the lips of Spike Nolan. Lean and rangy with a thin face, he was some five years older than his associate. A drifter from Wyoming, Jacob

Taggart had taken him on to help with the spring round-up. Nolan was astute enough to recognize which side of the street was sunniest and had quickly latched onto the young whelp. As the rancher's son, Corby had plenty of dough to throw around.

The kid was hot-headed and arrogant. But for Nolan, such an attachment definitely had its compensations. Free drinks on a Saturday night, the best lays upstairs at the Blue Chandelier Sporting House, not to mention a brand-new Henry repeater. All had come Spike Nolan's way.

Ever since the elder brother had returned though, Corby had been like a bear with a sore head. Glowering at everyone, he constantly picked arguments on the slightest pretext. Nolan felt as though he was treading on eggshells whenever the kid was around.

Corby had voiced the resentment he had against his elder brother in no uncertain terms to his new *amigo*. Nolan had just listened. Family squabbles were none of his business. And criticizing the boss's elder kin was not a good move.

'He ain't a patch on you when it comes to workin' the ranch,' continued Nolan trying to hold the middle ground. 'And the boss is bound to leave it to you when he pops his clogs.'

'You reckon?' snapped Taggart, skewering his buddy with a frigid glare. 'Wouldn't put it past the old coot to leave the whole shebang to that ass-lickin' brother of mine.'

It was early Saturday evening. The two cowboys were hunched over their drinks at the bar in the Blue Chandelier. The saloon was just beginning to fill up. In the corner a tinny piano picked out a popular ditty of the day.

Smoke hung in the air, yellow and static in the dim light cast by a pair of smelly tallow-lamps.

Corby hawked a gob of phlegm at the brass spittoon. He missed. All round, the raucous clamour of Saturday-night revelry washed over his head, unheeded and ignored. Spike eyed his companion, noting the twitch at the corner of his mouth, a sure sign that Corby was about ready to snap.

The kid banged his glass on the bar top. 'Another bottle over here, Joe,' he shouted. His voice was beginning to slur as the hard liquor took effect.

The bartender nodded awkwardly. There was no way he wanted to get into an argument with Jacob Taggart's son. Hurriedly he served a customer before produced a new bottle of bourbon. But a tight-lipped gesture to the kid's *compadre* warned of impending trouble in the not too distant future. Nolan responded with a curt nod. He understood.

Corby had already sunk more than his fair share of Red Label bourbon. And it was clear to the other drinkers that the young cowpoke was out for trouble. They recognized the signs. The curled lip, the narrowed eyes devoid of feeling and coldly staring into the mirror behind the bar. Like a disturbed sidewinder, his right hand kept fingering the Remington New Model Army revolver tied low on his hip. Nobody wanted to meet that lurid gaze.

Slowly, so as not to attract undue attention, the other drinkers shifted along the bar.

Nolan waited, nerve ends strung tighter than a whore's corset, the black moustache twitching nervously. He slung back another shot and refilled his glass, the fiery liquor burning a path down into his stomach.

Breathing deep he said, 'It ain't Link's fault that he's the clever one.' Immediately he regretted the remark.

'Meanin' what?' challenged Corby, turning to face the older man. The cutting rasp brought a grey cast to Nolan's craggy features.

'Every man has to plough his own furrow,' he added quickly. 'Link's more at home behind a desk, whereas you've gotten talents that are more practical.'

Corby emitted a tight grunt. But the reply seemed to satisfy the young hot-head. Nolan breathed a sigh of relief.

'So why don't the old man treat us both the same?'

'Maybe he figures that he does.'

'He allus favoured Link, ever since we was kids.' A dark shadow, sombre and malicious, played across Corby's smoothly youthful features. 'Well, the time has come for him to realize that I won't be pushed around no more.' He belched loudly, slamming a bunched fist down on the bar.

Then Nolan repeated his original question.

'So what yuh gonna do?'

Corby heaved himself off the bar.

'You'll see,' he hissed, jabbing a finger at his friend. 'I aim to get even with that old bastard. Nobody plants his brand on Corby Taggart like he was some stray maverick.'

Squaring his shoulders, he grabbed the full bottle of bourbon and lurched towards the door of the saloon. Without any thought, he barged straight through a group of revellers prancing about in the centre of the room.

'What the hell you doin', feller?' ranted one angry carouser whose female partner had been unceremoniously bundled aside.

As on previous occasions when his friend had rubbed people up the wrong way, Spike Nolan was left to step in

38

and pour oil on troubled waters, mollify and appease what might become an ugly confrontation.

'Don't mind him,' he apologized, helping the flustered lady to her feet. As on previous occasions, he placated the irate punter with a couple of dollar bills which he stuffed into the fellow's pocket. 'He's too drunk to know what day of the week it is.'

The saloon gal accepted Spike's hand, then gave him a coquettish smile.

'What about me then, feller?' she said, both hands provocatively placed on her swaying hips. 'Don't I merit some recompense?'

'Sure thing, ma'am.' Spike kept himself between the girl and her current beau as half a dozen more bills were poked into the lady's bulging cleavage.

'Much obliged, cowboy,' she purred with a sly wink. 'Be seein' yuh around sometime.'

Spike remained silent but his gleaming lust-filled eyes assured the girl that he would certainly be holding her to that promise. After all, hadn't he paid up front?

The man huffed some but the proffered restorative assuaged his blustering protestations. With a nonchalant tip of his hat to them both, Nolan thanked the man for his forbearance, then hurried off after the disappearing rebel.

Threatening storm-clouds had brought darkness early to the streets of Cimarron. The moon, unable to make its presence felt, had given up and gone home. Balls of tumbleweed scuttled down Main Street, egged on by a stiff wind. So far the rain had deigned to hold off. But for how long?

Somewhere in the distance a dog barked. Light from

the street coal-oil-lamps flickered behind their glass screens, rather dimmer than usual. Everybody was inside, having taken shelter from the expected downpour.

The street was empty. Or so it appeared.

Then a lone shadow appeared, flitting along the boardwalk. Rather hesitantly, it kept stopping in doorways, peering about anxiously to ensure nobody was aware of its presence.

As the elusive image passed one of the sputtering sources of illumination, it was transposed into a face cast from granite. Eyes gritty and resolute peered from beneath hooded brows casting a gaze of implacable determination. The normally slack mouth had tightened. The youthful contours were angular and set firmly on an immutable track.

For Corby Taggart, there could be no turning back now. Tension clutched at his innards. He wasn't scared. But this was the first time he had actually set out to deliberately flout the law, even though to his warped thinking it was justified.

He stopped outside a large mercantile store scowling at the legend emblazoned across the window – *Taggart's Saddlery and Cattlemen's Emporium.*

Thin lips split in a tight smile. But there was no humour displayed. For somebody intent on mischief, tonight was perfect. And Corby had every intention of taking full advantage of that fact.

Inside the store, Dan Hardrock Forester was totting up the day's takings. An old cowhand now well into his sixties, he had been with Jacob Taggart right from the start. And the rancher had rewarded his loyalty by placing the old-timer in charge of the store once riding the range had proved too much of a chore.

Corby assured himself that apart from the store-manager, the place was empty. A couple more hard draws on his stogie to settle himself, then he threw the smouldering butt to one side.

As he made to step forward a panicky squeal broke the turgid atmosphere. It was instantly accompanied by a sharp sizzle of burnt fur. A damn blasted cat. The animal shook off the unexpected assault on its person, then shot away beneath the boardwalk leaving the young felon to stifle his jangled nerves.

He waited a few more minutes to gear himself up once again.

Then, setting his hat low over his forehead, Corby removed the yellow bandanna from around his neck and secured it across the lower half of his face. Only his crystalline-blue eyes showed. And by adopting a gruff tone of voice, there was no way that old Dan would recognize him.

Purposefully, he drew the Remington from its holster and checked the loading. A brief nod confirmed that all was in order before he gave another quick scan up and down the dimly lit street.

Then he quickly opened the door and stepped inside, remembering to pull the blind down and slide the locking bolt across.

FIVE

THE POT
BOILS OVER

'Put yer hands in the air and don't make no sudden moves,' growled Corby, waving the revolver at the surprised storekeeper. 'This is a stick-up.'

Hardrock Forester's mouth dropped open. This was the first time he had come up against a thief. But the old-timer was no milksop.

A life on the open range had seen to that. Not to mention a spell in the state penitentiary in his younger days for shooting up a saloon down in Silver City. By itself a minor offence, but two men had died during the fracas. Hardrock had made no secret of the dent in his character when signing on for Jacob Taggart's first cattle drive up the Sedalia Trail back in '66. And Taggart had respected his honesty. The two had remained firm friends ever since.

The storekeeper's thick grey moustache bristled with indignation. Nonetheless, he stood back from the counter and raised both his hands.

'Now shovel all that dough into a sack and hand it over, pronto!' jabbered the intruder.

'Sure thing, mister,' drawled the storeman, carefully eyeing the young hardcase. 'Anything you say. Just keep that shooter under control.' He held up a placatory hand, sensing the bandit's jumpiness. Dan Forester had no wish to end his days with his boots still on.

As he filled the gunny-sack with banknotes, he eyed the young tearaway warily. His brow puckered in thought. There was something about him that registered. It was there at the back on his mind, niggling away. He just couldn't figure out what it was. He knew the kid was putting on a rough accent to make himself appear older, more experienced in the ways of conducting a hold-up than he actually was.

Keep him talking, thought Hardrock. Maybe something would click.

'You from around these parts?'

'Come on, Forester,' snapped Taggart, ominously waggling the pistol. 'Quit stallin' and hurry it up. I ain't got all night.'

The kid was sure edgy. Not only that. How did he know the storekeeper's name? The dude must hail from this part of the territory. He kept throwing a furtive gaze towards the street, listening. And each time, that yellow neckerchief masking his face flapped about like a loose wagon tarp.

That was it. The yellow bandanna.

Recognition struck the old cowboy right in the brisket like he'd been kicked by a loco mule.

Corby Taggart.

The jasper facing him was the boss's younger son.

43

He had given the kid that very same bandanna as a birthday present some five years back. Obviously young Taggart had forgotten. But Dan Forester certainly hadn't.

Hardrock's eyes bulged. His whole body tensed.

Taggart noticed the old man's abrupt change of manner.

'What's eatin' you then?' His enquiry emerged as a high-pitched bark. It would have been almost laughable if the implications weren't so critical.

'Think I don't recognize yuh . . . Mister Taggart?' prodded the storekeeper, fixing the kid with a weighty stare.

Corby's thin face blanched.

'W-what yuh t-talkin' about, old man?' stuttered the robber, clearly rattled by this unexpected revelation. 'Don't know anybody by that name. Now hand over that loot if yuh don't want a gutful of lead.' But the attempted bravado lacked any vigour.

Forester responded with a harsh guffaw. Quickly he grabbed the sack of money and shoved it under the counter.

The intruder bridled at the unexpected resistance.

'What will yer pa think if he finds out his own kin is a common thief?' he reproved, stepping slowly round the counter. His hawkish grey eyes held those of the intruder in a mesmeric embrace. 'Now you hand over that gun nice and easy-like, and I'll pretend this never happened.' His hand lifted expectantly.

'You keep away,' exclaimed a rapidly panicking Corby Taggart. This wasn't how it was meant to be. He was meant to be the one giving the orders, the one in control. 'Come any closer and I'll shoot.'

Forester scoffed. 'You ain't gotten the guts, kid,' he

jibed, a contemptuous sneer matching the harsh cut. 'Now hand over that pistol, and be right quick about it.'

Taggart backed away, his finger raking back the revolver's hammer.

'Keep back, I tell yuh!' He was almost crying. His gun hand trembled dangerously, the trigger finger whitening as it began to squeeze. Corby Taggart had passed the point of no return.

Alarm bells were ringing. The store-manager should have read the signs in the kid's frightened eyes, his shaky voice.

Still Forester came on, his right hand reaching for the deadly barrel that was pointing straight at his body.

In the corner the clock chimed the half-hour. It was 9.30 p.m.

The sombre tolling was the final straw. It signalled that the kid had reached his breaking point.

'I told yuh not to crowd me,' he yelled as the trigger was hauled back.

The gun exploded. Thick smoke filled the room as the thunderous crash resounded between clapboard walls.

Hardrock Forester uttered a terse grunt, staggering back under the impact of the .36 shell. His left hand clawed at the burst of scarlet pumping from the chest wound. The fleeting notion passed through his dimming brain that he had gravely underestimated young Taggart, and was about to pay the ultimate penalty. Floundering like a stranded trout, he lurched against a pile of tools, scattering them in all directions. Then he sank to the floor on both knees before keeling over onto his face.

A pool of blood, dark and terrifying, seeped from under the still form.

Corby Taggart was disorientated, stunned. Shocked into immobility by the bizarre scene facing him, his mouth hung open. The saturnine look registered nothing but a blank acknowledgement of the heinous crime he had just perpetrated. As the smoke cleared, however, a dull realization slowly but remorselessly filtered through to his addled brain that he had killed a man. Shot him down in cold blood.

This was not how it should have been. The storekeeper was supposed to have shrank back in terror whilst Corby scooped up a sackful of greenbacks, and hightailed it back to the ranch with no one any the wiser. That would have wiped the smile off his father's arrogant puss.

As things stood, here he was facing a murder rap and a one-way trip to the gallows. And it would be just like the old bastard to have Link conduct the case for the prosecution.

That was when his mind began to function again. A furtive spangle, cold as a March blizzard, glinted in his shifty eyes. His lip drew back into a tight smile.

Hardrock Forester was dead. So apart from himself, there were no witnesses to the killing. All he had to do was make certain nobody saw him leave the store and he would be high and dry, in the clear.

There was no time to lose. Cimarron was prey to all manner of gunplay at the weekend when cowhands from all over the county converged on the town. But it was Wednesday night. And a stray gunshot was more than likely to find the town marshal hot-footing it down the street to find out what the hullabaloo was all about. In fact, he could be here at any moment.

Corby hustled over to the door and peered through the

window. The street was still empty. He thanked the approaching storm for that. Quickly he sidled out onto the boardwalk, paused for a second to listen, then slipped mutely down the adjoining alleyway where his horse was tethered. Exhaling loudly as his taut nerves slackened off, Corby Taggart savagely dug his silver spurs into the cayuse. The sooner he put distance between himself and Cimarron the better.

It was the pounding of iron-shod hoofs at the gallop that first attracted Jacob Taggart's attention. It was an hour after sun-up and he was having breakfast in the study which overlooked the main corral of the Box T. A design feature incorporated into the ranch house, it enabled the boss to keep track of the comings and goings of his employees.

The big man pushed a half-eaten plate of eggs and bacon aside and stood up. Such a sound would not normally have produced the blunt grimace that now creased the rancher's ribbed features. But this was the rhythmic beat from a single cayuse, and one that was clearly in a hurry.

Quickly he stepped over to the large picture window and peered out.

Chuck Holliday reined up in a cloud of yellow dust, almost tumbling out of the saddle in the process. Known to one and all as 'Slow Hand' on account of his easy-going manner, the marshal's uncharacteristic haste brought an added measure of concern to the rancher's dour expression.

Wiping the grease from his mouth with a napkin, Taggart hustled down the wide stairway to greet the new arrival.

As he tugged open the heavy oak door, Holliday was already halfway up the garden path. He appeared flustered, the rotund girth wobbling like a pair of unfettered breasts. The down-at-heel range garb was dust-shrouded and more unkempt than usual. On perceiving Taggart framed in the open doorway, the marshal's pace faltered, his left eye twitching. Nervously he pulled at the drooping grey moustache that sought to conceal his wizened leathery features. Drawing the crisp morning air deep into his lungs, the lawman then continued.

This was not a meeting that he relished.

'Howdie there, Slow Hand,' greeted the rancher maintaining a false air of sanguinity. 'And to what do I owe the pleasure of your company at this early hour.'

Holliday coughed. It was a tense, uneasy gesture, a stalling tactic to give him time to consider his response. This was certainly no pleasure trip.

Facing each other across the six feet of wooden veranda, the two men couldn't have been more different. Both were hovering around the mid point of their half century, but there the similarity ended.

Tall and dignified, the stoic rancher exuded an aura of authority. Even at this early hour he was clad in a black suit tailor-made in Santa Fe. His iron-grey hair was still thick, the upright bearing still lean and muscular. Here was a man who had worked hard to achieve his position in the community, and who would strive equally hard to retain a solid grip on that success. And woe betide the man who would challenge that claim.

But Jacob Taggart had known the marshal for many years. He knew that the laid-back indolent persona was a guise, a quirk that gave the lawman an edge. It was a character trait that Chuck Holliday actively encouraged. On more than one occasion Taggart had witnessed the uncanny speed and accuracy with which the law officer had dispatched adversaries who had challenged his authority on the streets of Cimarron. Many were now permanent residents in the town's cemetery.

'Seems a mite early for you to be up and about,' pressed Taggart.

Holliday removed his hat.

'I could sure use a cup of coffee,' he drawled, stepping up onto the veranda.

'Coming right up,' announced the rancher, struggling to keep the edginess from his voice. He knew that Holliday could not, would not be rushed. Ushering the lawman into the wide hall, he called for a pot of coffee and hot biscuits to be served in the den at the rear of the house.

It was a further ten minutes before the marshal eventually got round to explaining the purpose of his visit.

'Is Corby around?' he asked over the rim of his coffee-cup.

Taggart's muscles stiffened, his whole body went rigid.

'Ain't seen him since yesterday afternoon.'

'Where is he now?'

'Far as I know, he's out on the north range. Been there all night with Spike Nolan rounding up strays after the storm.'

'There's questions I need to ask him,' hedged the lawman uneasily.

'What's this all about, Chuck?' Taggart was losing his patience. His voice held an jittery note of irritation. 'If Corby's in trouble then I want to know.'

Holiday's face assumed a hard frosty aspect. This was where things got tough.

49

'Fact is, Jacob . . .' He paused, stood up and walked over to the window. The sun had chased away the early mist that usually hung over the valley. Meadow-larks twittered as a new day geared itself up. The tranquil scene failed to inspire the lawman. He had other things on his mind. Slowly he turned, facing the rancher square on. 'Fact is . . . Corby has been accused of armed robbery.'

Taggart's jaw dropped. His face blanched.

'But that can't be so,' he protested, leaping to his feet once the shock had registered. 'No son of mine would commit any such crime.'

'I've gotten the proof,' continued Holliday undaunted. 'But I'm afraid it's a lot more serious than that. He shot Hardrock Forester, and the doc says he's unlikely to pull through. That means your son could be facing a murder charge.'

'Hardrock!' exclaimed Taggart in a hoarse croak. 'Murder!' He was barely able to comprehend what he was being told. His legs felt like jelly. He staggered over to a chair and slumped down. Trying to summon up a measure of defiance he shot back, 'What proof have you got that it was Corby? He wouldn't be stupid enough to just mosey into the store and gun down the old-timer.'

'Remember that yellow bandanna he often wore? The one that old Hardrock gave him for his birthday some years back.'

Taggart nodded blankly.

'Well he had the thing masking his identity. Forester recognized it.'

'Could have been anybody wearing that,' scoffed Taggart. 'Neckers are a dime a dozen.' But the retort lacked bite.

'How many yellow bandannas have you seen in these

parts, Jacob?' snorted Holliday. 'The old guy told me he had it specially brought in from Santa Fe.'

Taggart had no answer to that. His shoulders slumped. In ten minutes he appeared to have aged ten years.

'Did he take anythin'?'

Holliday shook his head. 'Must have panicked then lit out fast.'

The rancher swung on his heel to conceal the hurt, the humiliation that suffused his sunken features.

The die was cast. He was now forced to admit that his son was a sneaking thief, and, like as not, a killer as well. Taggart's thick eyebrows knitted together. He stepped over to his desk and poured himself a generous slug of Scotch whisky, downing the contents in a single gulp. The sole reaction was a slight reddening of the cheeks.

This dire revelation needed thinking on. It had left him jaded and weary. For five minutes he sat in the large swivel-chair behind his desk, just staring at the far wall, his eyes flat and lifeless.

It was the marshal who broke into his torpid reverie. With a discreet cough he said, 'Seein' as how Corby ain't here, I'll leave it for you to bring him in.' He fixed the rancher with an intent look. 'You will do that, won't you, Jacob?' he pressed, setting his hat straight ready to depart. 'I don't want to have to come out here again with a warrant for his arrest.'

'Don't you worry yourself, Slow Hand,' answered the rancher in a lacklustre voice. 'I'll do the right thing.'

But he didn't elaborate on what that might entail.

'I'll be off then.'

Holliday waited for an acknowledgement. But the rancher had already turned away, dismissing him.

*

'What happened then?' Beartooth Crockett fervently expressed his curiosity regarding his companion's stirring revelations.

The two men had broken camp and were heading west offering their backs to the rising run. After voicing a condensed chronicle of his life story, Link had fallen silent. His raw-boned features held a serious frown. During the narration, Crockett had listened quietly, nodding occasionally but voicing no comments, nor expressing any opinion. He felt it best to allow his young companion to unburden himself in his own way, and at his own pace.

But the bizarre account had wetted his appetite for more. Such were the consequences of living alone for months on end. Mountain men were inveterate gossipers. At the annual rendezvous, the tales were many and varied, becoming ever taller as the rot gut disappeared down liquor-starved gullets.

'Was your brother arrested?'

Crockett's hesitant query failed to register with the pensive lawyer. The trapper shrugged, spurring ahead down a grass slope on which grew the occasional pine and aspen saplings. At the bottom was a lake, bordered by broad-leaved cottonwoods. The narrow deer trail followed the left hand edge of the lake, whose placid waters flawlessly reflected the rising backdrop of rocky ice-towers.

Crockett reined to a halt and allowed his mount to drink her fill whilst enabling his sidekick to catch up.

Link drew to a halt beside the buckskinned trapper and gazed into the blue waters that gently lapped the ochre shingle.

He went on with his narration. It was as if he had never stopped but had merely taken the briefest interlude for a breather.

'I was on the way back to the ranch from my office in Cimarron when I met up with Holliday on the trail,' said Link, patting Smudger's head. 'The guy never gave me any intimation of what had passed between him and Pa. He said it was just a social call.' Link uttered a harsh laugh. It was more of a terse, biting grunt. 'I sure found out the grim truth when I got home.'

SIX

WYOMING BOUND

It was five hours later when Corby Taggart returned at last to the Box T. Announcing his presence with a raucous whoop and a tinkling of the silver-conchoed reins he favoured, the younger Taggart swaggered into the entrance hall of the ranch.

'I managed to get them stray mavericks branded and corralled,' he announced briskly. Removing his leather gloves and slapping the dust from his Levis, he continued, 'Took me most of the night though.' Corby licked his dry lips. 'Sure could use a jugful of that lemonade. My mouth feels like sandpaper.'

Silence.

Corby began to sense that something was wrong.

He peered closer. His father was standing in the middle of the room, his back ramrod-straight. But it was the riveting black expression of pure repugnance that caused the young rannie's heart to falter. To his left, Link shuffled his feet uneasily. Surely they couldn't know about the robbery. Forester was dead.

At last Corby's father spoke. The words boomed out, echoing around the polished oak-panelled walls.

'Where were you last night?'

Corby's breathing was ragged. Somehow he managed to keep the guilt-induced waver from his reply.

'You know where I was,' he countered firmly, holding Jacob Taggart's icy glare with the greatest effort, 'Out on the north range. Hunting out those strays from the brush. And it was damned hard work as well.'

'You're lyin'!' The vigorous retort blasted out like a cannon shot. 'You was in town after robbin' the store. But things didn't work out, did they?' Taggart hurried on, fury causing his voice to rise noticeably. 'Old Hardrock wouldn't play ball so you shot him; gunned down one of my oldest *compadres* in cold blood.'

'What yuh talkin' about?' spat the shaken kid. 'Ain't I just told yuh? I was out on the range.'

With an agility born of pure anger, Jacob Taggart sprang forward, grabbing at the damning evidence round Corby's neck. At the same time, a stinging back-hander struck the youngster hard across the mouth.

The kid yelled, blood pumping from a split lip.

'Don't deny it,' howled Taggart, violently shaking his younger son. 'Here's the evidence agin yuh. You were recognized 'cos of this necker. How do you think I knew what happened?'

Link sensed that in such a foul temper, his father was capable of anything. And being a qualified lawyer, he knew the consequences could be equally severe for both father and son should the situation be allowed to get out of hand. That was no answer. Quickly, he intervened to prevent further injury to his brother. Charily yet with deft resolve, he eased the two apart.

'This needs talking through,' he cautioned. 'No sense in going off half-cocked.'

Still fuming, Jacob nonetheless allowed himself to be steered away.

Corby slumped against the wall dabbing at his injured mouth with the offending piece of cloth. The truth was out. The question dogging his chaotic thoughts was, *who had split on him?*

The puzzled frown drew a harsh chortle from the simmering rancher.

'Wonderin' how come I know all about this, ain't yuh?' he snapped, sinking another Scotch. Without waiting on an answer, he continued: 'Old Hardrock lived up to his name. The poor old guy may have been gut-shot, but he survived to scupper your blamed scheme. And now the law wants its pound of flesh.'

Corby's mouth dropped open.

'Forester's still alive?' he exclaimed.

'He sure is,' cut in Link. 'But only just. The marshal doesn't think he'll last the week out. So if he dies, which seems likely, you're facing a murder charge.' In a more conciliatory, almost sad tone, he then added: 'Why did you do it, Corby?'

The kid lurched to his feet, a snarl creasing the youthful complexion. He dragged an arm across his bloodied face.

'Pa allus favoured you, put you on a pedestal.' He let out a scornful grunt of derision. 'The great Lincoln Taggart—'

'You cut that out,' rapped the old rancher, slamming a balled fist on the desk. 'Didn't it enter that thick skull of your'n that it was you who would have inherited all of this.' He flung out his arms to encompass the sumptuous surroundings. 'Lincoln with a successful law practice. And you running the Box T. Now you've gone and ruined all my plans.'

As quickly as it had burst forth, the fight went out of the rancher. He suddenly felt his age, an old man at the end of the road. Then he peered askance at his younger son. A spark of pity, maybe even understanding flickered in the rheumy eyes. Had he been too harsh, too strict with the kid? Ever since Abby had died of the fever, it had been his responsibility to raise his sons.

With Lincoln it had been simple. No problems. The elder boy had toed the line, done as a good son ought to do. But Corby was a different proposition. Headstrong and ornery, he had constantly balked at the leash.

Just like his pa.

Jacob Taggart allowed a brief smile to play across the strained contours of his leathery skin.

Corby was kin, his own flesh and blood. There was no way he could allow him to become gallows-fodder.

'You gonna turn me in, Pa?' croaked the disconsolate young gunslick.

Taggart eyed him disdainfully.

'I'm goin' for a ride up onto the south rim,' he announced, ignoring the doleful question. It was the place to which he always went when there were matters that required pondering over. The site where his wife was buried.

In moments like these, Jacob Taggart felt the need of her wise counsel. Standing up, he settled the pearl-grey Stetson squarely on his head. 'I'll be a couple of hours,' he said. A new resolve oozed from his taut frame. Striding purposefully over to the door, he turned adding laconically: 'Try not to rile each other while I'm away.'

'Sure, Pa, no problem,' replied Link with an optimistic note he did not feel.

Corby merely wrinkled his brow, offering a quizzical frown as he speculated as to what the old guy had in mind.

It was approaching sundown when Jacob Taggart eventually picked his way down from the fractured sandstone mesa known as Segundo Bluff. Silhouetted against the purple backdrop, he sat tall in the saddle. There was a steely glint in his eye, a tightness about the jaw that intimated a decision had been made.

Through the rest of that day, the two riders made steady progress towards the head of the valley. By mid-afternoon, they were climbing a boulder-strewn gully in single file. On either side, towering pinnacles of flaking rock punched at the sky. Chunky banks of cumulus scudded by overhead, egged on by a stiffening wind.

Then, all of a sudden, as if a curtain had been drawn back, there it was.

The log cabin lay beneath the sheltering protection of an enormous rocky overhang at the back of a wide grass ledge. Away to the west stretched another valley with a mighty sheet of plunging foam at its far end.

'Heartbreak Falls,' announced Crockett proudly, pointing the Hawken towards the silvery outflow. 'And beyond. . . .'

Link gasped. There, framed in the gap, above and beyond the awesome cataract, he could clearly discern the rounded profile of the missing Sugar Loaf. Its summit was

58

caked in a bluish sheen of ice. Truly a mouth-watering spectacle.

For five minutes, both men just sat their mounts, and stared at the inspiring tableau. It was a first for Link, but Jubal Crockett was equally transfixed. Even though he had witnessed the spellbinding vista on many occasions, his reaction was always the same. That was one of the reasons he had chosen to make his life in the Upper Yellowstone.

It was Crockett who broke the easy silence.

'I've left written instructions in the cabin,' he drawled softly. 'Whoever buries me when I go to meet my maker should have the grave laid face on to the Heartbreak – right next to that of White Dove so's we can enjoy the view together.'

The trapper's poignant utterance brought a lump to Link's throat. Even though he had been raised a towns-man, Link could well understand the big man's sentimen-tal attachment to this wild yet beatific and romantic locale.

Eventually he broke the spell.

'Is Moose Jaw on the far side?'

'Sure is,' replied Crockett with a questioning frown aimed at his companion. 'We'll set out in the morning. The trip should take us no more'n two days.'

The cabin was spartan, reflecting the simple and some-what monastic life of a solitary trapper, although he had made some attempt to make the place more homely by covering the bare log walls with fur skins and beaded Indian artwork. There were also numerous intricately carved wooden figurines dotted around.

Later that night after supper Crockett again prompted Link to resume his story. They were seated facing the stone hearth, one with the customary pipe, the other hauling on a stogie. The trapper could barely contain himself. He was becoming ever more curious as to how and why this young man from New Mexico had found himself in this remote wilderness of north-west Wyoming.

'That brother of your'n musta bin one skittish young tearaway,' observed the mountain man settling back in his favourite rocking-chair.

Link sat opposite.

Fully relaxed following a hearty meal of freshly caught trout with home-grown squash and potatoes, a snug contented glow suffused his entire being. Perhaps it was the home-brewed liquor. Coupled with the warmth from a crackling fire in the grate, he felt strangely at home here in the mountains. It was as if destiny had led him here.

He threw a smirk towards his gargantuan host, then nodded slowly before resuming his story. Not that there was much left to tell.

'Pa was mad as hell with Corby. But the kid was still his son.' The shadows cast by the firelight caught the intensity of Link's impassioned gaze as he spoke out. 'When he eventually returned to the ranch, he was once again the tough, hard-nosed pioneer of old. The pig-headed son-of-a-gun who had braved Indians, rustlers, famine and drought to create a thriving beef bonanza.' Link smiled at the recollection.

There was only one solution to the dire fix that his equally mulish son had gotten himself into.

'First thing come daybreak,' he announced brusquely, addressing the young hothead, 'I want you on the trail. Out of Colfax County and New Mexico.'

Corby was stunned. His father had always been a stick-

60

ler for the law. Yet here he was offering his son a way out.

The old man didn't wait for a reply.

'I'm sending you to stay with my brother in Thermopolis, Wyoming Territory. He operates a livery business out there. It'll give you the chance to make a fresh start.' Taggart fixed a steely eye onto his wayward offspring. 'And don't be thinkin' you can just disappear. I'm havin' Clancy Balloo go with yuh. He knows that territory like the back of his hand. And I can trust him to get you there in one piece.'

Balloo was a leading hand who had been with Taggart since they first pushed up the trail from Texas. He would make sure the kid reached his destination.

'In that case, can I have one of my own pards go with me?'

Taggart squinted uneasily.

'Who've you gotten in mind?'

'Spike Nolan and me are good buddies,' pressed Corby. 'If I'm steppin' out into unknown territory, I could do with a friendly face around.' His smooth features bunched into a twisted grimace. 'That Balloo ain't exactly a barrel of laughs.'

Taggart's own face took on a vibrant tinge redder than a setting sun. His moustache bristled indignantly. 'This isn't meant to be no picnic, yuh young whelp,' he shouted. 'Stay around here and it's a necktie party for sure. You're my kin and I have a duty to stand by yuh. But don't you dare treat this as a joke, y'hear? I'll have a lot of explainin' to do when Holliday comes out here again. And I have to convince him that you skedaddled afore I could bring you in.'

'S-sure, Pa,' stammered Corby. 'I'll do whatever you say.'

Taggart then curtly dismissed his son with orders to go make his preparations for the journey.

Corby left the Box T at first light accompanied by Spike Nolan and the stalwart figure of Clancy Balloo, who had a pack-mule in tow. It was an unobtrusive farewell. Only Link was there to wish his younger brother godspeed. None of the other hands had been made privy to the arrangements. As far as Taggart was concerned, the fewer people who knew about this sorry business the better.

The rancher remained out of sight. But as the two riders spurred out of the corral heading north for the Colorado border, a curtain stirred in an upstairs window. A solitary tear etched a path down the seamed contours of a face haggard with grief. Alone in his room, Jacob Taggart succumbed to his anguish, wallowing in self-pity.

Would he ever see his younger son again?

'I take it that your brother wasn't at Thermopolis when you arrived,' stated Crockett, topping up their tin cups from a fresh jug of moonshine.

Link shook his head.

'He had moved on. Uncle Johnny said he hadn't taken to life working in a livery stable. Reckoned mucking out stalls was beneath him. His view was that Corby was heading for trouble. The kid spent most of his time in the saloons. When my uncle challenged him about his slack attitude, Corby took offence and told him to stuff his job. He left the next day. Said he was going to try his luck in Moose Jaw.'

'That so,' drawled Crockett sinking further down into his chair. But he was only half-listening. The moonshine was having a soporific effect on his concentration. Soon they had both fallen asleep in their chairs.

A further three days passed before they were able to head west towards Moose Jaw. The restless storm-clouds that had been threatening during most of the previous day finally made their presence felt. Heavy droplets of rain soon coalesced into a heaving downpour. Unrelenting and continuous, the howling tempest rampaged across the mountainous landscape augmented by frequent jolts of forked lightning.

Never had Link experienced such ferocity. Brilliant flashes fizzed and crackled between the jagged peaks. Clamorously supported by a legion of cosmic drummers pounding away high up in the firmament, the sight was indeed awesome to behold.

Crockett had seen it all before. He had built the cabin to withstand such onslaughts.

He took advantage of their enforced incarceration to teach his young companion some of the skills needed to survive in the mountain wilderness. Stripping and preparing a beaver-pelt, creating a suit of clothes from deerskin, cooking a feast fit for the president using forest herbs.

And most important of all, acquiring a sense of direction.

Once they had parted company his guest would have to find his own way back to the dubious pleasures of civilization. Link was an eager pupil, although he knew that he could only hope to absorb the bare rudiments of what had taken Beartooth a lifetime of living in the wilderness.

Eventually the storm deigned to release its stringent grip on the landscape of Beartooth Creek and they were able to leave. What could have been a wearisome three days had proved to be eminently profitable and enlightening. In some ways, Link was sorry to leave.

But he had a task to fulfil, and the sooner the better.

Jigging their mounts across the grassy shelf, Link turned to his companion and said, 'I never did tell you the reason for my being here, did I?'

Crockett raised a drooping eyebrow. He also had overlooked this key question.

'Plumb forgot all about that,' he chortled.

'The storekeeper had hovered on the brink,' Link continued. 'In and out of consciousness. Between the devil and the deep blue sea. One minute the old guy was lucid and talking, the next sweating out a fever and teetering on the edge.'

'What did the marshal do when he found out your brother had skipped the territory?'

'He was mad as a wild bronc. But there was nothing he could do. Pa just claimed that Corby had lit out, and he had no idea where he had gone.' Link shrugged. 'It put a strain on their friendship. No question. They haven't spoken since. But kin is kin.' He looked askance at the other rider. 'You have to look after your own, wouldn't you agree?'

'I got no argument with you there,' concurred the mountain man.

'A month after Corby left the Box T,' Link went on, 'we learned that old Hardrock was tougher than anybody had imagined. He pulled through. The doc reckons he'll be right as rain in a few months. No more sneaking over to the ranch on his day off to help bust them wild broncs though.' Link chuckled at the notion. 'Pa had him brought over to the ranch where he's given the old-timer a room until he's fully recovered. So that's why I came out here. To find Corby and take him back.'

'Won't the kid be a mite touchy about havin' to face an attempted murder charge?'

'Being a lawyer, I reckon I could get him off with a couple of years in jail.' Link's face creased in a pensive frown. 'It's better than being on the run for the rest of your life and having bounty killers on your trail. Me and Pa agree that a brief spell in the pokey will do him a power of good.'

Crockett appeared sceptical. His mouth curled in a wry twist. He scratched his greasy mop.

'If it was me,' he said, 'I sure wouldn't be too keen on the idea.'

The mood became sombre as Link reflected on a possible turn of events he hadn't bargained for.

It was on a particularly steep section no more than a hundred yards from the cabin that the accident happened. Crockett had negotiated the rock step a thousand times before. Perhaps his mind was still on the recent conversation with his young companion as the dangerous twist in the trail was reached. The reins were held too loose as the cayuse hit the bend at the trot and stumbled.

Taken completely unawares, the trapper was thrown from the saddle. He hit the ground with a heavy thwack. A loud crack echoed between the solid rock walls of the ravine. There was no mistaking that ominous sound. And Crockett's right leg bent underneath his body at an ungainly angle told both men in no uncertain terms that the limb was broken. The trapper winced as an agonized barb of pain lanced through the shattered leg. It felt as though he was being jabbed by a hundred red-hot needles.

Instantly, Link threw himself out of the saddle and dragged his *compadre* back from the edge of the trail over which he was hanging. Another couple of feet and he would have been tossed over the lip into oblivion. A tortured howl of anguish broke from Crockett's mouth as the injured member jarred beneath him. Sweat coated his tanned brow, his bulky torso heaved with shock.

He cursed volubly. 'Serves me damn well right for not keepin' my eyes open.' Another excruciating stab pulsated through his body. He stiffened, his face creasing with the pain. 'What have I been tellin' yuh about keepin' up a healthy respect for the mountains? And I go and let this happen.'

'It was my fault,' apologized Link, 'I shouldn't have distracted you.'

'There ain't no excuses for a knuckle-headed bozo like me gettin' hisself distracted.' Crockett lambasted himself vehemently. His dark eyes glittered with self-reproach. 'Some tough mountain man I am.'

There was nothing Link could say to ease the big guy's humiliation. All he knew was that he had to get the injured man back up to the cabin. It was a good job they hadn't ridden any further. He shuddered to think what the consequences would have been then.

Gently he helped Crockett to his feet.

'Take hold of the reins and hang onto the saddle,' he said, arms supporting the wobbling man. 'Can you manage to hobble back up the trail on your good leg? It's not far, thank the Lord.'

Crockett gave a curt nod and gritted his teeth.

The broken leg hung uselessly dragging on the rough ground. Each step was sheer agony. But the trapper was determined that not a sound would pass his lips. It took them a half-hour to cover the one hundred yards back to the cabin. Crockett slumped onto his bunk gasping for breath like a landed trout. He grabbed at the jug of moonshine and tipped a hefty slug down his throat.

Half the contents had disappeared before the intense pain began to subside, dulled by the numbing effect of the powerful liquor.

'You're gonna have to set the leg,' slurred Crockett, his eyes watery and half-closed. Having been brought up on a ranch, Link had acquired some experience of setting the broken bones of injured animals. A human could not be very different. Straightening the twisted limb was the last straw for Jubal Crockett. His mouth opened in a silent scream. Then he passed out.

Link gave a sigh of relief. He was able to clean the open wound and reposition the protruding femur before setting it in splints. Tying off, he nodded with satisfaction. Although it would be a month at least before Beartooth Crockett could sit a horse for any length of time.

That was when he realized that he was going to have to make the journey down to Moose Jaw alone.

It was the following morning before Crockett finally surfaced. He stretched tired and aching muscles. Thankfully the moonshine had allowed him to sleep for a full twenty-four hours. The pain in his leg throbbed abominably, but at least it had been well set.

'Sorry about this, Link,' he apologised sheepishly. 'You make sure to come back this way when you find that brother of your'n, yuh hear?'

'Don't fret none, Beartooth. I aim to see you up and riding before I light out back for New Mexico.'

Crockett smiled. That was what he had hoped to hear.

'Take heed of what I taught yuh and yuh should reach Moose Jaw tomorrow night.'

They shook hands, then Link spurred off down the trail.

A raucous peal of laughter followed his back.

'Mind that rock step now!'

Link raised his hand in a rude gesture, a thin smile playing across his tight features. In minutes he had reached the step. He reined up and paused. Only then did he look round. Crockett was leaning on a crutch framed in the cabin's open doorway. Their eyes met briefly. Then Link turned to concentrate all his attention on surmounting the awkward hazard.

SEVEN

KID SILVERS

Right from the start, Spike Nolan had realized that the kid was heading for the owlhoot trail after he had bragged about shooting down old Hardrock Forester. The kid had quickly shrugged off the initial shock of making his first killing when he realized that his father wasn't about to hand him over to the law. The cowhand had no qualms about accompanying his buddy to Wyoming. It was just another job. And Taggart had paid him double the normal rate in advance.

The problem had come when Corby somehow managed to get rid of Clancy Balloo. Nolan had his own ideas as to how the so-called accident had occurred. At the time, they had been riding in single file along a narrow trail through Colorado's Medicine Bow range north of Denver. On their right was a soaring cliff face. The trail itself followed a stony ledge no more than six feet in width. On the left was a sheer drop of several hundred feet into a ravine of broken rocks and scrub vegetation.

Head bowed under the buffeting wind, Nolan had his

hat pulled well down. He was in the lead at the time, allowing his mount to pick its own route. Next thing, a cutting
scream rent the ether. He spun round in the saddle.
Balloo had disappeared over the rim of the canyon. Man
and horse had gone in an instant, plunging headlong into
the abyss amidst a tumble of loose boulders and dust,
never to be seen again.

'What in thunder happened?' gasped Nolan, eyes
bulging in disbelief.

'The nag must have lost its footing,' tossed back the
younger man almost carelessly. He gave a casual shrug.
But his eyes were merciless chips of flint, granite hard and
icy cool. Nothing had been said, but Nolan knew in his
heart that the kid had deliberately panicked the other
man's mount. He had obviously just been biding his time
for the right moment, the killing stroke.

Balloo had always been his father's man. A trusted Box
T hand. Almost like a spy ready to report back every little
incident to the boss.

Now that that constraint had been lifted, there was
nothing to stop Corby Taggart from going his own way.

As it was, they had headed for Thermopolis. Corby had
figured on getting a grubstake from his uncle. And then
heading west. Spike Nolan had no reason not to tag along.

From then on, Corby had insisted on being called Kid
Silvers. And why not? With the number of conchos on his
vest and hatband, it was an appropriate handle.

Since leaving Thermopolis, the Kid's gun hand had
spoken a further three times. On two of those occasions,
Nolan had been forced to step in and help his buddy out
of a tight corner. Now he also was well and truly on the
wrong side the law. He had little doubt that Kid Silvers was

enjoying the nascent reputation which he was building up.

They had come across Patch Montana on the trail to Branson Forge.

All on his ownsome, the little guy had held up a stage-coach and was trying to persuade the passengers to hand over their valuables. He was dancing round the coach like a demented puppet, the gun clutched in his tight paw threatening to erupt at any moment.

Silvers and Nolan had hidden behind some rocks close by to observe the proceedings. The pair had been much amused by Montana's rather inept attempt at highway robbery. Being on the receiving end of the clumsy robber's gun, the passengers had been suitably cowed by the little guy's frenzied ranting. Not so the driver, who recognized a ham-fisted amateur and intended to boost his standing with the stage company by capturing a poten-tial road agent.

So when Patch unwittingly presented his blind side, the driver saw his chance to draw a bead on the robber. Silvers had figured that this was the moment to intervene.

Levering a shell into the Henry carbine, he had called out, 'Just ease yer finger off the trigger, pilgrim. Assumin' of course yuh want to keep that head on your shoulders.'

Patch and the driver both looked towards the sudden interjection.

When Montana saw that the gun was not pointed at him, he yipped and heehawed with glee.

'You heard what the man said,' he hollered, waving the pistol. 'Drop the gun.'

The driver, sullen and crestfallen, realized he had lost the advantage and that no job was worth a bullet in the brisket. The gun hit the dirt in double-quick time.

'Now you folks inside,' clucked Patch, removing his derby. 'Just place your goods in the hat and you can be on your way.'

'You won't get away with this, baby-face,' snapped the driver as he was preparing to whip up the team of six. 'I'll have your snivelling mug on wanted posters all over the territory.'

Nolan took a deep breath.

The Kid detested being reminded of his youthful looks. He had grown a moustache solely to give him more presence, more authority. And calling him *baby-face*. That was like teasing an irate sidewinder. Spike Nolan clicked his tongue, knowing what was coming next.

A rabid snarl of anger erupted from the Kid's throat. His pugnacious jaw trembled. Then three shots from the Henry blasted the driver clear off his seat, from which he fell, splayed out over a clump of prickly pear. Silvers immediately leapt to his feet and berated the deceased man as blood poured from the fatal wounds.

'Nobody insults Kid Silvers and gets away with it.'

His next remark was to a dazed Patch Montana. Along with the passengers, the diminutive robber was rooted to the spot in shaken bewilderment. 'Seems like me and my pard have done you a favour, mister. Don't that deserve a share of the loot?' Patch merely nodded vacantly. 'Come on then,' guffawed a highly elated Kid Silvers. 'Time we was splittin' the breeze.'

Soon the bizarre trio were hightailing it away from the grisly scene of their first real hold-up.

When Silvers reckoned they had put enough distance between themselves and the robbery, he called a halt. It was late afternoon and there was no way they would reach

Branson Forge that night. Leading off the main trail into a hidden draw, he ordered Patch to brush out their sign.

'No sense in takin' chances,' he said in response to the newcomer's quizzical frown. 'You never know who might happen along.'

Over a makeshift supper of refried beans and sour-dough biscuits, Patch voiced the notion that had been bugging him for some time.

'You fellers got plans then?' he asked casually, shovel-ling the orange mess down his gullet. His beady peepers squinted over the tin plate.

Silvers puffed contentedly on a cheroot.

'We're aimin' to have us a share of the lucre that's been discovered on the Yellowstone,' he warbled airily. 'Ain't that the case, Spike?'

Nolan replied with a brief nod. 'Sure is. But without all the hard graft.'

Silvers uttered a hearty chuckle at his sidekick's witty riposte.

'An extra couple of pards would make things a heap easier, don't yuh think?' A nervous cough followed Patch's hesitant submission.

Silver's eyed him warily.

'What yuh gettin' at, mister?' The brittle retort was steely, edged with suspicion.

'Me and my brother are both eager to join up with some companionable jiggers. Fellers what know the score, and ain't afraid to crack open a few eggs, should the need arise.' Patch Montana paused to assess the Kid's reaction. Silvers was staring at him. It was a frosty glower, frigid with scepticism. His right hand had slid down to caress the polished butt of his sixgun. The signs looked bleak and gloomy. But Patch pressed on. 'We're both handy with a gun,' he averred.

'Ever killed a man?' The question was uttered in a flat monotone.

'Two,' came back an immediate rejoinder. 'Both using a Bowie.' He tapped the ten-inch sheathed blade on his left hip. 'Best way when you're rollin' drunks. Trouble is, there ain't no future in it. A few dollars here and there. Peanuts. I wanna join an outfit that's goin' places.' A leary smile cracked the grimy façade. 'Like your'n. The Silvers Gang!'

A dreamy cast played across the Kid's youthful face. His smooth cheeks bulged in a half-smile.

The Silvers Gang!

Yep! It sounded good. Had a certain ring.

A tense silence enfolded the campsite. All eyes were fastened onto the Kid.

'The Silvers Gang,' he murmured, gently rocking on his haunches. 'Maybe I could use a couple more *compadres*.'

'You won't regret it, Kid,' gushed an over-ebullient Patch Montana. 'I'll back you all the way. You can rely on me.'

The Kid shot him a piercing frown.

'What about this brother of your'n? When do we get to meet him?'

The colour drained from Montana's face.

'Well,' he began diffidently, whilst rubbing his stubbly chin. 'That's what I was about to tell yuh.'

'Spit it out!' growled Silvers acidly.

'He's bein' held by a bunch of wranglers over at Lockjaw Canyon. His nag had gone lame when we came across this herd of wild broncs they was bustin' for the army. There was nobody about at the time, so he moseyed on down to take his pick whilst I kept a look-out. We'd been up all night after bein' chased out of Jackson. What with the heat an' all, I fell asleep. Next thing, all hell breaks loose. Fellers shootin' and hollerin' like mad fiends.'

'Get to the point,' rapped Silvers.

'Zeke had been caught red-handed.' Patch untied his necker and dabbed at his brow. 'Makes me all of a sweat just thinkin' on it,' he remarked, gulping down a slug of hooch. 'You fellers know what they do with horse-thieves?' The question was rhetorical. He hurried on. 'They was all fer stringin' him up there and then.' Patch took a breather and another slug of whiskey, sagaciously nodding at the recollection.

'So what happened?' enquired Spike Nolan avidly. He was totally enthralled, gripped by Patch's vicarious revelations.

'It was the boss man, a army guy with three stripes who stopped them. Claimed that because they was workin' for the army, everythin' should be done by the book. He sent a couple of the wranglers back to Jackson to fetch the sheriff.'

'So what d'yuh expect me to do about it?' railed Silvers, jumping to his feet. He knew what was coming.

'The three of us would have no trouble breakin' him out of the cabin,' pleaded Montana. 'Once the wranglers have left to hunt some more horseflesh. Oughta be a cinch.'

He peered at the two outlaws hopefully.

'What d'yuh say then?'

'I say you must take me for a right sucker,' snapped Silvers, grabbing Montana and hauling him up off the floor. The Kid's left eye twitched angrily. 'Spin us a fancy yarn about wantin' to join a sound outfit. And all you was after was us freein' up your goddamed brother.' He shook Montana until his teeth rattled. It was only the forceful intervention of Nolan that prevented the Kid from doing the little man some permanent damage.

'It ain't like that, Kid, honest,' implored Montana. 'I swear on my mother's grave.'

Silvers scowled, cursing vehemently. 'A runt like you ain't got no mother.' But his quick fire temper was already dissipating.

He threw Montana aside and set his mind to thinking.

Eventually he spoke, having come to a decision.

'This better be on the level,' he warned. ' 'Cos if you're dealin' from the bottom of the deck—'

Montana interrupted the threat of retribution with his own brisk assertion that everything he had said was the truth.

Early next morning, with the new dawn filtering out the blackness of night, the three outlaws broke camp. Nolan tipped the coffee dregs over the fire.

Streaks of pink and lilac were spearing the eastern sky as they jigged their mounts towards the distant prominence of Sublette Peak. Starkly etched in flaming orange against the rapidly swelling backdrop, it marked the western extremity of their objective, Lockjaw Canyon.

The corralling pens which caged in the herds of captured mustangs were at the far end of the box canyon. A two-roomed shack had been constructed to house the wranglers. Tacked onto the end was a lean-to. According to Patch Montana, this was where his brother was being held. He led them in single file down a narrow trail at the closed end to avoid being spotted. Exposed blocks of

76

orange sandstone hemmed them in on both sides where a savage rent had been torn in the canyon's back wall.

'Doesn't look as if there's anybody about,' observed Nolan squinting his eyes against the new day's sun.

'They could be inside the cabin,' commented Silvers with a cynical twist of his lower lip.

Eager to please his new sidekicks Montana suggested stampeding the mustangs in the corral. 'That oughta bring 'em out if they're in there.'

Silvers nodded. This little runt wasn't all solid bone between the ears. He turned to Nolan. 'We can wait behind that clump of rocks down there.' He pointed a gloved digit at the chosen place of concealment. 'Soon as them jiggers are clear, we head down and get this guy out.'

Nolan gave a curt nod of understanding.

'Check your hardware,' ordered Silvers, drawing his own weapon and spinning the cylinder. Then, holding each of them in a tight gaze, he added, 'But no gunplay unless it's absolutely necessary.'

Montana disappeared amidst the chaos of tumbled boulders. Keeping out of sight he circled behind the cabin. Nolan saw him emerge on the far side and slide the two holding poles from the entrance to the corral. Creeping wraithlike to the rear of the corral, he removed his hat and began slapping it onto the rump of the nearest mustang. Taken unawares, the cayuse reared up on its hind legs and leapt forward.

The unexpected movement instantly caused panic to set in amongst the rest of the feisty broncs. In a flash they were bolting headlong through the open gate.

The ground shook as the stampeding horses headed towards the mouth of the canyon. If there was anybody inside the cabin, this would surely bring them scurrying out to investigate the disturbance.

And it did. Three men clad in long johns emerged hurriedly, tugging on their boots. As soon as they realized the nature of the uproar, they saddled up and bit the dust. That was the cue for Kid Silvers and Nolan to hustle across the open sandy clearing to release Zeke Montana.

The heavy plank door of the lean-to was only secured by an outer bolt. Silvers was just about to slide it back when a brusque rap split the ether.

'Don't neither of you turkeys move a muscle.' The gruffly coarse rasp came from behind. Silvers' hand automatically fell to the revolver on his hip. 'Touch that smoke-pole and you is dead meat, mister,' rapped the tetchy voice. 'Now turn around slow and easy so's I can get a good look at yuh.' The man chuckled to himself. 'Seems like it'll be a triple hangin' for the boys to enjoy when the sheriff gets here.'

'I don't think so.'

The wrangler was given no time to figure out that he'd been wrong footed. The blooded point of a ten-inch Bowie knife stuck out of his midriff. On the other end, Patch Montana gripped the bone handle. Twisting the blade, he hauled it clear wiping scarlet globules on his greasy Levis.

The sickly grin that screwed up Montana's face matched the merciless glitter in his black eyes. A vein pulsated in the bullish neck as the buzz of having just killed a man thrust to the fore.

Spike Nolan inwardly cringed. The little runt had actually enjoyed the experience, relished it. The cowpoke hadn't figured on his association with Corby Taggart deteriorating to this gruesome level. He had heard tell of men becoming addicted to killing. This was the first time he had witnessed the phenomenon at first hand.

Spike knew he was no angel. Sure, he had killed himself, but only in the line of duty, so to speak, when it was absolutely necessary. Maybe it was about time he lit out for pastures new, before it was too late. The Kid's ogling puss, slavering like a bitch on heat, was a reminder that such a course of action would require careful planning if he was not to end up like this poor guy.

Patch toed the wrangler's still twitching corpse aside and dragged open the door of the lean-to. Tentatively he peered inside. A fetid odour of rotting vegetation assailed his bulbous snout.

'Anybody in there?' he hollered.

A grizzled visage appeared in the opening. Zeke Montana's face was swathed in a black straggly beard, his matted hair caked in dried blood. It was clear that he had been on the receiving end of a severe kicking prior to his incarceration. A bloodshot eye, purple and swollen, squinted at his three rescuers. The other was completely closed.

'That you, Patch?' he croaked, the hoarse enquiry filtering from between mashed lips. 'Man, I sure am glad to see you.'

The little guy sucked in his breath, then stuck an apelike arm around his brother's waist and helped him out of the hovel.

'Give me a hand here,' he barked at Nolan.

Momentarily, the attention of the three desperadoes was fixed on the injured horse-thief. It was Silvers who sensed a movement to his left; a brief shadow flicking across the corner of his vision.

Without thinking he dropped to the ground, swinging and drawing his revolver in a fluid arc of mind-boggling speed. Flame and death belched forth slamming the intruder back against the cabin wall. It was the army sergeant. A dark blotch rapidly spread across the front of his blue tunic. The revolver slipped from nerveless fingers.

'Shoulda . . . let the boys . . . hang yuh,' he gurgled, sliding down the wall.

'Too late now, soldier boy,' cackled Patch Montana, eagerly drawing his own pistol.

'Let me have the pleasure of finishin' the bastard off,' hissed his brother, pushing forward unsteadily.

Patch handed over the cocked Navy. 'Be my guest, big brother,' he cawed.

Snarling like an enraged bull, Zeke Montana pumped the entire cylinder into the dying man.

It was Nolan who brought the gloating outlaws back to the reality of their situation.

'The sound o' them shots will have carried down the canyon,' he rapped tersely. 'Time we was hittin' the trail pronto afore them jiggers figure out they've been tricked.'

It was a clear night. The wind had dropped to a faint hush. Overhead, a shimmering moon bathed the clearing in its soft glow, laying a bold emphasis on the shadowy terrain. Flat slabs of rock angled down into the meandering snake of Blue Nose Creek beside which stood a lone grey canvas lean-to. The dwindling embers of a fire gave the darkness a red tinge.

'You figure he's inside, Corby?' asked a hatchet-faced jigger, palming his revolver.

The man being addressed was much younger with a

smoothly boyish complexion. He glared at his sidekick, jabbing him in the ribs.

'How many times have I gotta tell yuh,' he hissed in a menacing tone. 'That name's from a past I wanna forget. It's Kid Silvers now. Savvy?'

Patch Montana sucked in his breath. He was a short stocky dude sporting a black covering over his left eye.

'Sorry, Kid,' he mumbled, 'It just slipped out.'

'Well, make damn sure it don't in future.'

On his other side, Spike Nolan was carefully studying the campsite. Nothing moved. They had left the fourth member of the gang to watch their horses and keep an eye on their back trail.

The Kid scanned the clearing, his eyes screwed almost shut.

'Looks as if he's alone,' he muttered, 'Just like we figured.'

'This'll be like takin' candy from a baby,' grunted Montana, stepping out from the cover of the rocks in which they had been crouched. The double click of the Navy Colt's hammer seemed to echo round the clearing.

All three froze, listening for any sign of movement.

Only the low, even murmur from the creek broke the silence.

Silvers drew his own sidearm. 'You come in from the far side,' he said to Nolan. 'I'll drag open the tent flap and get the drop on him.' His curt order to Montana was for the little man to keep back and cover them. Even though the young firebrand had a look of the greenhorn about him, he had a ruthless streak and was a mean-eyed jasper. And he was no slouch when it came to settling arguments. The Army Remington did all the talking. . . .

*

Carefully, the three hard-boiled robbers crept catlike across the clearing towards the tent. Silence held the landscape in its tender embrace. For now.

When Silvers was satisfied that they were in position, he whipped open the tent flap and poked his gun through the opening.

'Don't make a move else I'll drill yer,' he yelled.

A startled yelp came from the interior, followed by a panicky scuffling.

Two shots rang out across the dark enclave as flame belched from the Kid's revolver. A choked scream pierced the oppressive silence.

'I told yuh not to move,' howled the Kid, pumping another two slugs into the inert body. His eyes gleamed a fiery red, the thin lips drawn back in a manic grin.

'Give me a drink!' he hollered at nobody in particular.

Nolan stuck a bottle into the outstretched hand. The Kid drank deep and long, gasping as the hard liquor struck the back of his throat. It felt good, helping to soothe his fevered brain. It was always the same after a killing.

Once recovered from the initial shock of gunning a man down, the oddly assorted trio of owlhoots ransacked the camp searching for the gold they were sure was there. After half an hour, all they had uncovered was a small leather poke containing barely a handful of the gleaming dust.

The Kid snarled.

'Is that all?' he growled, the black orbs rolling back into his head.

Montana could only shrug.

'Maybe he's hidden it,' he chirped.

'That ain't no use,' ranted Silvers. 'It could be any place.'

'No sense in hangin' around here,' butted in Nolan. 'This'll have to do 'til we can figure out our next step.'

Silvers balked at the proposal but was forced to concur. Though he was determined that next time, things would be different. No more heading out on some wild-goose chase without determining all the facts. He grabbed the poke from Montana and stuffed it inside his shirt. Soon they were jigging their mounts away from the grim scene heading back towards Moose Jaw.

EIGHT

MOOSE JAW

The sun was rapidly sinking behind the craggy peaks of the Absarokas. Black and gauntly surreal, the mountains stood proud against the brazen luminosity of the fiery sunset. It was three days since Link had left the cabin in the Upper Yellowstone. He knew that he ought to have hit Moose Jaw the previous evening.

For the second time in as many weeks, he knew that he was lost.

So where had he gone wrong? He cursed aloud.

Once again he was beginning to question the wisdom of travelling alone through this bleak and unforgiving land.

But it seemed that a guardian angel was keeping the young tenderfoot under her protective wing. The trail he had been following for the last few hours suddenly opened out as the trees thinned to expose open grassland intermittently dotted with spruce and aspen.

Sandwiched between the river bend and a rocky bluff stood a cluster of single-storey buildings. The main one boasted a large wagon wheel above the entrance porch. On its right was a barn and corral containing half a dozen horses, with a blacksmith's shop to the left. Maybe he was nearing Moose Jaw after all.

A grey-haired man appeared in the doorway of what looked like a general store. He was tall and rangy and sported a battered old hat curled up at the brim. A thick black belt supported a pair of brown corduroys.

Link didn't slacken his pace. He was only too pleased to have arrived at his destination. Only when he reached the veranda did he haul up, tipping his hat to the older man.

'Howdie there, friend.' He smiled. 'I sure am glad to have reached Moose Jaw at last. Figured I had strayed off the trail and gotten myself lost again.'

A wide grin cracked open the rancher's grizzled visage. He slapped his thighs, hooting with laughter.

'Hey, Marcy,' he called to someone inside the building, 'Come out here and listen to this.'

A young woman of around Link's own age emerged from the house, dusting some flour off her apron. She was clearly in the midst of preparing the evening meal.

'What's all the fuss about, Dad,' she complained, 'I'm in the middle of kneading the dough for that apple-pie you been nagging me about all week.' It was then that she took heed of their unexpected visitor. A red tinge suffused the girl's alabaster cheeks. Quickly she removed the apron and smoothed down her dress. 'Why didn't you tell me we were having a guest for supper?'

The man ignored the girl's flustered warbling.

Again a throaty chuckle broke from deep within his broad chest.

'Listen to this, daughter, and quit yer gripin'. This dude figures he's reached Moose Jaw. What d'yuh reckon to that then?'

'Moose Jaw!' the girl exclaimed, her mouth flapping open. Link couldn't help but note that even beneath the floured exterior, she was a comely female and no mistake. 'He thinks this is Moose Jaw?' she repeated.

'Sure does,' hooted her father. The notion had certainly tickled both their fancies. A scruffy grey hound of a tarnished aspect not dissimilar to that of its master acknowledged the joshing with a ribald howl.

Link was quickly arriving at the conclusion that he had not in fact arrived at his destination. He felt decidedly foolish in front of the girl, more so because she was no ugly duckling. Even beneath the dull grey working-shift, he couldn't help but note the trim shape. A mite boyish perhaps, but there was no denying she was a woman. And a bright pink ribbon tying back her long auburn hair confirmed the effort to maintain some degree of femininity, even out here in the wilderness.

'I take it this is not Moose Jaw,' he offered rather lamely.

Again the rancher uttered a raucous cackle. This story would be recounted at the monthly barn-dance for years to come.

Smiling coquettishly, the girl revealed a set of perfect white teeth. 'You missed the turning back a-ways up the trail. It's easily done. So don't feel too embarrassed.' Then she gave her father an admonishing glower. 'Take no notice of Pa. He don't get much chance to exercise his chuckle muscles out here in the boondocks.'

Link felt his burning cheeks revert to their normal tanned hue. This girl clearly had a way of putting strangers at their ease.

With some effort, the rancher managed at last to control his hilarity.

'The name's Brett Waggoner,' he announced, holding out his hand, 'and this is my daughter Marcy. You've stumbled upon the Wagon Wheel Trading Post and this is the Huckleberry Valley. Moose Jaw is a day's ride to the south.'

Link accepted the firm handshake. 'Link Taggart from Cimarron down New Mexico way,' he replied.

Waggoner reined in his amused gaze, offering the younger man a new degree of respect.

'You've come a long way, Mr Taggart. All things considered, it maybe ain't surprisin' that you've strayed off the trail. 'Specially in country like this.' Like all frontier settlers, he didn't press Link for an explanation.

'I reckon Mr Taggart has done a real swell job of getting this close to his destination,' interrupted Marcy Waggoner, adjusting the hair-ribbon whilst flicking a speck of flour from her dress. She had just realized how dowdy she must look to this handsome stranger. 'Supper's about ready if you want to join us,' she said from beneath lowered eyebrows. 'Its only beef-stew and dumplings, but you're more than welcome to what there is.'

'Not forgettin' the apple-pie,' reminded her father.

Link quickly removed his hat. 'That's much appreciated, Miss Waggoner.' His head bobbed like a cork on water.

'You can wash up at the well over yonder, if'n you've a mind,' said the storekeeper pointing to a cast-iron pump beside the corral. 'And there's plenty of feed for your cayuse in the barn.' Link nodded again, then swung Smudger away from his new companions.

More than ever, he was coming to appreciate the spellbinding attraction of the Yellowstone country, and not only for the quality of the scenery.

*

Kid Silvers and his disparate crew were in the Last Chance saloon on Moose Jaw's main street. Once a boom town, it was now well past its heyday. Gold had been discovered in the lower Yellowstone some ten years previously. But it was only a minor strike. The initial euphoria that had attracted prospectors from far and wide had soon dissipated. Of the mining towns that littered the valley bottomlands, only Moose Jaw had survived. The rest had rapidly been swallowed up by the insatiable appetite of nature.

The town was fortunate in that it was situated at the junction of two valleys where the respective trails converged. Some of the older residents still managed to scrape a living from their claims but the rewards were meagre and those with an eye for the 'main chance' had moved on to pastures, or diggings, new.

Silvers was reflecting on the sad fact that he had arrived too late. The rapidly declining contents of the leather poke brought a sour grimace to his smooth visage.

'How much we gotten left?' enquired Spike Nolan in a sombre tone.

Silvers fingered the small flat sack.

'Enough to set us up in a new game.' The Kid threw back his tumbler of whiskey whilst aiming a sceptical leer towards a nattily attired dude playing solitaire in the corner. 'I can feel it's my lucky night.'

'You said that yesterday,' grumbled Patch Montana, casting a jaundiced eye at his sidekick. The Kid had lost most of the poke in a single game. Patch could almost see the gambler rubbing his hands in anticipation.

Silvers stiffened. His cold eyes narrowed to thin slits. Before Montana realized, a gun barrel was prodding his veined snout.

Nolan looked on sardonically. He was in the owlhoot game now whether he liked it or not. And the Kid did have an eye for sniffing out easy targets, most of the time. It was just that, of late, his judgement had been rather off course.

'You wanna take over this outfit, Patch?' he growled, staring flint-eyed along the glinting metal. 'Maybe you figure I ain't up to the job?'

The corpulent outlaw's piggy orbs bulged, sweat-beads bubbling on his forehead. Holding his pudgy hands out to forestall any precipitate action on the Kid's part, he backed off, mumbling an apology.

'Patch didn't mean no offence, boss,' rumbled Zeke Montana. 'It's the drink that's talkin'. Pay him no mind.' He had gladly joined the Silvers gang following his rescue from Lockjaw Canyon and had every faith in the young hardcase to make good on his boast that a life on easy street was just around the next bend in the trail.

Silvers grunted, gave a quick jolt of the shooter up Montana's left nostril then leathered his gun. Scowling, he splashed another slug into his glass.

At that precise moment a lyrical cadence broke through the Kid's mordant cogitations. It was followed by a tug on his shirt-sleeve.

'I couldn't help hearin' you fellers talking about missing the boat,' warbled a throaty voice to his left.

Silvers peered down on a shortish guy propping himself up on the bar with a crutch beneath his right shoulder. Further investigation revealed the jasper was sporting a wooden leg. An angular, bewhiskered skull gave him the likeness of a grinning mouse, a similarity compounded by the close-set beady eyes and pointed nose.

'What you blabbin' about, mister?' snapped the Kid,

clearly irritated by the interruption. 'I don't cotton to eavesdroppers. Now get lost before I lose my temper and forget you're a . . .' He paused for effect, aiming a derisive glare at the little fella '. . . a cripple.'

Peg-Leg Carver was nothing if not persistent. He came straight to the crux of the matter. His gruff voice lowered to barely more than a whisper.

'You was gripin' about there bein' no gold anymore in these parts.' Carver focused his attention on the baby-faced jigger. He was clearly the boss. Then he said, 'Well that's where you're wrong, mister. And I can lead yuh to it. Lots of it.'

Silvers' lip curled. He snorted. But his interest had been aroused.

'And why would you do that for complete strangers,' he scoffed, trying to inject a measure of scepticism into the rebuff.

Carver flicked his cadaverous head towards the end of the bar as he back-hobbled away from the other drinkers. The outlaws followed automatically. Hunched shoulders were raised, their crestfallen demeanour suddenly became more animated.

'OK!' snorted Silvers, 'What's your angle?'

Carver peered around furtively. Nobody was paying them any heed. The bartender was busy polishing glasses; the gambler had corralled a new herd of suckers to fleece; and the other drinkers were too engrossed in their own problems to pay old Peg-Leg Carver any mind. That was, unless he had had a good week on his claim. Only then did his 'friends' emerge from their holes to shake his hand, and accept his generosity.

This particular week had not been one of Peg-Leg's

more lucrative periods. Indeed the lean, almost ascetic cast that composed his mottled features spoke of little in the way of profit for some considerable time past.

The old jigger had lost his leg in the war, courtesy of a rebel cannon at Chancellorville. He had made a small fortune during the first strike that had given the valley its name. But like so many others who had garnered riches beyond their wildest dreams, it had soon been dissipated in a wave of overindulgence. Now all he could manage was a small claim that paid barely enough to keep him in red label whiskey. He supplemented the meagre earnings by swamping out the saloon and collecting glasses.

Peg-Leg vigorously prodded a grubby digit at the offending stump.

'As you jaspers may have noticed,' he rapped, 'I ain't too lively on my pins no more. It means I can't get around like I used to. Whereas you boys look fit as fleas. Get my drift?' His eyes rolled up with a restrained hint of the ironic. 'So you can do the job I have in mind a heap quicker'n me. Then we split the proceeds, right down the middle. Half for me, half for you.' His world-weary features lit up expectantly. 'What d'yuh say then, boys? And remember,' he added knowingly, 'I've got me a contact who'll pay top dollar for every ounce of the yellow stuff I can produce.'

'And who might that be?' enquired Zeke expectantly.

'Now that'd be tellin', wouldn't it?' replied Carver, tapping the end of his protruding appendage. 'Not that I don't trust you boys. It just pays to be a mite cautious, that's all.'

Silvers sniffed then looked at his *compadres*, offering them a sly grin. He had no intention of letting Carver take half the lucre, giving his associates the other measly half to share between the four of them. But he would only let the old prospector in on the new deal when they had taken possession of the gold.

'What d'yuh say then, boys?' pressed Carver eagerly. 'Is it a deal?'

Silvers nodded. The old soldier spat on his palm and stuck it out. They shook.

'So where is this cache of loot?' prodded Spike Nolan.

'Not here,' muttered Carver, heaving himself off the bar. 'I'll explain the details back at my cabin. Now,' he enthused, grabbing a loose glass. 'How about a drink to seal our bargain?'

Link had not tasted home-cooking like this since leaving Cimarron. Simple fare it may have been, but nothing could beat victuals prepared by someone who knew their way around a kitchen. And Marcy Waggoner was certainly no novice in that respect.

She had learned the art of good culinary practice from her mother who had sadly passed away the previous summer. Like many of the women who had accompanied their families to a new life in the expanding Western territories, the harsh life and endless struggle to survive had fmally taken its toll.

The three of them talked well into the night. At ease in each other's company, they took delight in sampling numerous bottles of the French wine that Brett Waggoner had acquired from a passing drummer. He sympathized with Link's task of locating his brother, and couldn't suppress another burst of jocularity when the young man got around to mentioning how he had met up with Beartooth Crockett. The trader assured him that he would make it his business to keep tabs on the trapper's convalescence.

Link was more than pleased to accept the offer of a bed for the night.

Nestling down between clean sheets on a feather mattress, his final thoughts were of a silky-smooth oval face framed by flowing locks of shiny auburn, a smile that beckoned invitingly, and eyes of purest jade.

In his dreams, Marcy Wagonner's hauntingly mesmeric gaze dispatched an enchanting shiver through his whole body. Her gentle touch made his skin tingle. He could only trust that reality would be likewise encouraging. Once his mission was complete, Link vowed that he would make every effort to return to the Huckleberry.

Next morning, after a hearty breakfast, Marcy informed Link that she would be accompanying him to Moose Jaw.

'It's not because I think you'll get lost again,' she assured him with an infectious laugh. 'I travel there every couple of weeks to replenish supplies. A couple of days early will make no difference.'

Link was only too pleased to have such pleasant and alluring company. After making his farewells to Brett Waggoner, he saddled Smudger and set off on the ride to Moose Jaw.

'Now you make sure to come back and visit,' the trader called after his retreating back. Link gave him an enthusiastic affirmative in reply. He had every intention of so doing.

An undulating mist hovered above the highest peaks. Under the influence of the rising sun it soon dissolved. At this early hour, the gently pulsating warmth provided a relaxing tonic. Meadow-larks twittered and cavorted at play. A couple of rabbits chased each other across the clearing ahead. An idyllic scene. And with a lovely girl riding in the buckboard beside him, Link felt at peace with the world.

NINE

GOLD FEVER

Once Peg-Leg Carver had explained the location of the new source of gold in the Upper Yellowstone, Silvers and his crew wasted little time with the old prospector. The noxious stench emanating from his dug-out was enough to drive a skunk away.

'Don't forget we're partners,' Carver hollered at their rapidly disappearing backs. 'And it's me what can get the best price fer prime dust.'

Silvers waved in acknowledgement whilst offering his sidekicks a lopsided glower of derision. They sniggered in accord. Soon the four desperadoes were jigging their mounts back through Moose Jaw and up the tortuous trail that led back towards Beartooth Creek.

Carver had told them it was a two-day ride to where the gold-strike had been made. But Silvers was impatient. The lure of easy loot was infectious, like an aphrodisiac. They would eat and sleep on the move. Luxuries such as a cooked meal and the warmth of a campfire could wait until they had struck lucky. The sooner they had their hands on all that lovely booty, the sooner they could get to enjoying the high life for a change.

The other outlaws were imbued with the Kid's zealous air. Even Spike Nolan felt a new wave of optimism washing away the morose attitude he had adopted. Maybe he should stick around after all. Gold was an all-consuming enticement that few men could resist for long.

The Kid's heart would have skipped a beat had he known how near he had come to meeting up with his hated brother. It was only due to Marcy Waggoner's calling on a friend that she and Link had missed the fateful encounter.

The pair were jogging down Moose Jaw's main street barely an hour after the four outlaws had left. Link invited his delightful companion to dine with him at the best restaurant in town in appreciation for her kind hospitality. He was also loath to say goodbye to this girl who had so captured his heart.

Clear skies and a silvery moon played their part in helping the gang to maintain a steady tempo into the wild outback of the Upper Yellowstone. Silvers kept up an unrelenting jog-trot on the flatter stretches, taking regular peaks at the rough map that Carver had given him. But as the ground began to assume a steeper gradient, the gang was forced down to walking-pace. Chewing on sticks of beef jerky washed down with canteen water, even halts for the call of nature were denied them. Silvers was determined that this time, his ambition for a life on easy street would not be thwarted.

Around midnight they were climbing up the narrow trail that meandered tortuously into the wild and remote high country that marked the beginnings of Beartooth

Creek and the Upper Yellowstone.

Over to their right, the thundering cataract of Heartbreak Falls tumbled headlong from the confines of its own hanging valley. An awesome fount of white spume plunged unhindered for some 500 feet; even Kid Silvers was impressed. The stony mask momentarily slipped, involuntarily registering his amazement at this natural wonder. Taut muscles relaxed into a gaping stare.

Spike Nolan reined in his mount, likewise admiring the majestic sight.

'Now ain't that somethin' else,' he muttered.

That was enough for the Kid.

'Keep them nags movin',' he snapped, quickly reasserting his typically brusque manner. 'We've got more important things to think on. Damn water-spouts ain't gonna make us rich.'

It was another three hours of mind-numbing exertion before they eventually surmounted the infamous rock step and came in sight of the isolated log cabin occupied by Beartooth Crockett.

An owl hooted as the false dawn announced the start of a new day.

For the first time since leaving Peg-Leg Carver's dugout, Silvers called a halt. The others shifted uncomfortably in their saddles to ease cramped and protesting muscles. Only the Kid remained unaffected by the protracted journey. His eyes narrowed to thin slits as he scanned the area for any signs of life. Keeping within the cover afforded by the dense canopy of trees, he extracted a telescope from his saddle-pack and carefully surveyed the terrain.

The gentle rustle of a mountain breeze was all that disturbed the silence. Emitting a mournful sigh, it effortlessly stirred the reed-beds that flourished along the banks of the creek. The cabin was in darkness. If Crockett was at home, he must still be in the land of Nod.

That was the moment Zeke Montana decided to sneeze. Although stifled by a grubby bandanna, the raucous outburst elicited a snappy rejoinder from the Kid.

'What's with that durned racket?' he hissed, fastening a bleakly threatening eye on the culprit. 'You aimin' to let the whole valley know we've arrived?'

The curt reprimand produced a muttered apology.

'Sorry, boss. It's this mountain air,' he whined, 'It never did agree with me. Ain't that the case, Patch?'

'That's right,' concurred his brother. 'Zeke don't cotton to these high places. It gives him the—'

Silvers cut short any further entreaties the one-eyed weasel was about to offer on his brother's behalf with a brusque threat to his future chances of fatherhood should it happen again.

Not exactly the brightest button in the box, Zeke eyed the young hardcase sheepishly but knew when to hold his peace, and his itchy snout.

Luckily the sudden disturbance appeared to have passed unnoticed.

Silvers slid from the saddle. The others immediately followed suit, tethering their mounts to nearby pine-branches. His next remark was to Nolan. The steady gaze, coolly appraising, still remained locked onto the silent cabin frontage. Thin skeins of grey smoke drifted up from the stone chimney. Some jigger was clearly at home.

'You and Patch circle behind that clump of juniper and keep an eye on the rear,' he whispered. The words held a brittle edge, all the more puissant in the crisp morning air.

'I'll sneak round by the overhang and take him from the front. Soon as you hear me crash in through the front door, come a-runnin'. And fast! Got that?'

'Sure thing, Kid,' replied Patch as he and Nolan moved silently away to take up their positions.

'What about me, boss?' asked a chastened Zeke Montana.

Silvers aimed a flinty peeper at the hovering bruiser.

'You do what yer best at.'

Zeke frowned, his thick black eyebrows converging.

'Watch the nags and make sure they don't cause no commotion, like what you did. That is if'n yer able.' The sarcasm was lost on Zeke.

'Aw gee, boss,' he wailed dragging a hand through his tangled locks. 'Do I have to?'

The Kid's patience was rapidly ebbing away. He was beginning to have serious regrets about taking this lumbering oaf on. The clown was nothing but a pain in the butt.

'Just do it,' he snapped acidly. Once he had fastened onto the gold that old Carver claimed was just waiting to be picked up, he would ditch the whole caboodle and light out on his own. But until then. . . .

Link made it his business to have breakfast with Marcy Wagonner next morning. But once she had bought in the month's supplies, there was no further excuse for her to stick around Moose Jaw. So they said their goodbyes.

'You will call and see us?' she purred demurely from beneath lowered eyebrows.

The question was muted and rather too casually delivered to be a mere general enquiry. But a girl couldn't be too presumptuous. She had taken more than a passing fancy to this lawyer from New Mexico and sensed that he felt the same. Nothing had actually been said, and their liaison had been purely platonic thus far. Still, there was no harm in hoping.

Link assured her that he would call in to see her at the trading post once he had found his brother – or the trail had fizzled out. One way or another, this was going to be the end of the line.

They shook hands, eyes meeting hesitantly like two fluttering butterflies, fingers touching that fraction longer than formality demanded. When two people sense that something was happening between them, yet neither is quite sure what, their body language becomes stilted and wooden. They feel awkward in each other's company. But once they have parted, a yearning to take that next step becomes overwhelming.

Link Taggart knew now that he would move heaven and earth to reacquaint himself with Brett Wagonner's daughter.

But first there was a job that needed completing. He waited until Marcy's buggy had disappeared from view before setting about the fraternal quest.

None of the saloons in town had come across three cowpokes by the name of Clancy Balloo, Spike Nolan and Corby Taggart. Even checking the hotel registers proved fruitless. Sure, there were plenty of young kids passing through, and old guys in from the diggings. But nobody could offer any satisfactory information. Either that or they were keeping quiet.

Widening his search to visit the smaller settlements along the Yellowstone down as far as Shoshone Lake proved equally unproductive. Link was rapidly losing heart. His brother seemed to have completely disappeared. Maybe he hadn't even come this way at all.

Following another day of vague and futile responses to his questions, Link was sadly forced to admit defeat. He returned to Moose Jaw and acquired a pack-mule for the long trek back to Cimarron and the Box T. This time he was much more prepared. He knew the country and was determined not to get himself lost again.

Ears attuned to the slightest hint that the cabin's occupant was astir, Kid Silvers right hand tightened on the butt of his revolver. The rigid grip made his entire body tense up. Placing his left hand flat against the plank door, he prayed that it was not bolted from the inside. That would really upset the apple-cart. The Kid sucked in a deep breath. There was nothing to be gained by hesitating any longer. It was now or never. And the latter was unthinkable.

Girding his loins, he let fly a rabid war cry whilst resolutely pushing the door. It slammed inwards at his touch. Hustling through the narrow aperture, his squinting eyes panned the gloomy interior. There was a sudden movement over to his left.

Beartooth had always been a light sleeper. It was a product of being ambushed by renegade Indians once too often whilst scouting for the army. The instant that the cabin door burst open, he was grabbing for the loaded Hawken above the large grate. Had his leg been fully mended, he probably would have made it. As it was he fell awkwardly, the sudden movement dispatching a raw spasm through the stiff apendage.

'Keep yer mitts where I can see 'em,' snarled a rasping

voice. The speaker was jabbing the revolver in a threatening manner. 'And don't make no more sudden moves.'

Crockett stared up from the dirt floor into an oval
visage, smooth and boyish but sporting a thin wispy moustache. It was in sharp contrast to the pair of rough-looking
jiggers who had just entered behind him.

'If it's skins yer after, I ain't had chance to clean 'em
up,' he croaked through the waves of pain that creased his
injured leg. 'And as for a free breakfast, all you had to do
was ask. No need for all this hubbub.'

'Get him into a chair,' rasped the Kid, ignoring
Crockett's attempted banter. He threw a hank of rope to
Nolan. 'And tie him down real tight.'

Once the trapper was securely pinioned, Silvers
relaxed. 'We ain't after no mangy pelts,' he chided, poking
his shooter at their prisoner. 'It's somethin' much more
lucrative that we're after.' The red lips drew back in a
mirthless grin. 'Ain't that so, boys?'

Patch Montana nodded eagerly.

'And its gotten a lovely yellow colour,' cackled the one-
eyed hard-ass, prodding the sharp end of a Bowie at
Crockett's leathery face. Blood trickled from the nick.
Montana's scowling gaze fastened onto the tethered
captive. The bloated features screwed into a puzzled
frown. Something was bugging him. He had a vague
inkling of having met this bear of a mountain man once
before.

'So where's the gold?' pressed Silvers, hovering like a
predatory eagle. Both fists were balled, the knuckles
blanched white.

Crockett stiffened.

'Who told you there was gold up here?' he replied

curtly. 'I'm just a simple trapper. If there had been any signs of paydirt around here, I'd have found it.'

'You're lyin'!' The Kid's smooth cheeks turned a livid hue of purple. 'And if you wanna come out of this alive, you'd be well advised to spill the beans.'

The threat was immediately followed up by a solid right hook to the trapper's lantern jaw, followed by a series of savage haymakers. Crockett had no way of avoiding the lethal assault. His head slammed back against the chair back, blood pumping from split lips.

Silvers rubbed his bruised knuckles.

His next acid remark was aimed at Patch Montana.

'Go tell that brother of your'n to get his ass up here,' he balled. 'Seems like we need a bit more muscle to persuade this asshole to cough up the loot.'

Patch went to the door and signalled for his brother to join them.

For the next half-hour, the hulking bruiser did his best to batter the truth out of the stubborn trapper. But to no avail. Zeke was sweating with the exertion. This dude was one tough cookie.

Nolan had taken no part in the brutal assault. He was becoming more and more uneasy.

'Why don't you just tell us where it is?' His voice held a note of apprehensive concern. 'No sense in sufferin' when there's no need. We'll find the stuff in the end.'

'There is no gold,' repeated Crockett for the hundredth time. Lank hair hung down over his face. The cracked vocals, husky and raw, were barely audible, his battered face a misshapen mass of reddened lumps. Spitting out a loosened tooth, he croaked, 'And even if there was, I'd rather die than tell scum like you.'

'That can be arranged,' snapped Patch, closely eyeing the trapper. His thick brows were crinkled in thought. Where had he seen the guy before? 'So if you don't tell us, I'm gonna let my friend here loose on yuh.' He waggled the bone-handled knife in front of the sagging prisoner. The blade glinted in the flickering light cast by the fire.

And that's when Patch knew.

His single eye bulged outward. The ugly mouth twitched at the corners.

'Beartooth Crockett!' he yipped. 'I knew I'd heard that name afore.'

'You know this jigger?' asked Silvers rather lamely.

'Do I know him!' came back the animated exclamation. 'The bastard only did this to me.' His finger jabbed at his left eye. Savagely, he ripped the patch away to reveal an empty black socket, the edges ragged and hideously repulsive.

The Kid staggered back a pace. Even he was taken aback. Recovering his self-control, he asked, 'How did it happen?'

A manic howl erupted from the little guy's throat. He broke into a demented jig of triumph.

'Easy now, little brother,' cautioned Zeke.

But Patch ignored him. He had waited five long years for this moment. And he was going to savour every darned second.

'Figured you'd gotten away scot free, didn't yuh, mister? Well Jonas Montana don't forget. No sirree.' His head shook from side to side. 'I've dreamed of this moment. Every night since that day at Green River.'

Crockett peered up at the prancing hardcase through half-closed swollen eyes.

'Surely you remember, Mr Crockett.' Montana's tone had moderated to a whining lilt. Then, just as quickly the rasp hardened into a guttural snarl. 'Nobody forgets putting another man's eye out.'

'You gonna tell us what happened?' pressed the impatient gang leader. He wanted to get back to the business in hand.

'This turkey took offence at me pressing my claim to his woman. And a squaw at that.' The blunt-edged remark emerged as a scornful gibe. 'Far as me and my buddies were concerned, them red women were common property. This jigger thought different. There was a scuffle. He had a knife. And he used it.' He grabbed hold of Crockett's long hair and raised the drooping head. 'And I ended up like this. Well now it's my turn, mister.'

A baying shriek of rage and spittle spewed from the little guy's yammering maw. The huge Bowie quivered once then plunged. Its razor-edged point ripped into the trapper's left eyeball. The stomach churning squelch sounded like a grape popping. That was too much for Nolan. His guts erupted with a choking gurgle.

Crockett's mutilated body shook violently for a couple of second before he thankfully lost consciousness.

Apart from Nolan groaning aloud and clutching his heaving stomach, the others were frozen into shocked immobility. Even Patch Montana ceased his ranting and just stared open-mouthed at the knife, now grotesquely embedded in the victim's skull.

As always, it was the Kid who recovered first.

'Search the cabin,' he ordered bluntly. 'That gold has to be around here somewhere.'

For the next hour they turned the cabin upside down,

searching high and low for any gold that might have been hidden there. And their zealous endeavours did not go unrewarded. It was Zeke who made the discovery. And in a floor barrel of all places. Extracting a dust-coated leather poke, he tipped five small chunky nuggets into his hamlike palm.

'I've done found it,' he yelped excitedly sticking his paw under the Kid's nose. He was like the cat that got the cream. Now he would really be accepted.

Silvers grabbed the rough chunks of dull yellow and fondled them lovingly. So there is gold in the Upper Yellowstone after all, he thought, stuffing them into his pocket. He then picked up a bucket and went outside to the water butt. Returning, he flung the contents at Beartooth Crockett's recumbent body.

The shattered torso groaned, but did not move.

Silvers grabbed his hair and shook him awake. Pained croaks fizzled from between cracked and bruised lips.

'We've found the gold,' he snarled sticking the nuggets under the sagging head. 'So there's no point in holdin'' out on us any longer. Save yerself any more grief and tell us where the rest is.'

Crockett's mouth opened. He mumbled a confused response. But it was too garbled and incoherent for Silvers to make out.

'What did he say?'

It was Zeke who provided the literal translation.

'He said to go stuff them up yer ass.'

It was not what the Kid wanted to hear. His face turned ashen pale, cheeks puffing out with suppressed anger. Issuing a rabid growl, he instructed Patch to do his worst.

'An eye for an eye clearly ain't enough where this crowbait is concerned.'

Patch grinned malevolently, accepting the knife offered by his brother. But before he could do anything with it, two gun shots split the ether. Crockett's body jerked under the impact. The chair to which he was secured tipped over onto its side.

All eyes fastened onto the shootist.

'Why in hell's teeth did you do that?' railed Silvers.

'I've had enough,' replied Nolan keeping the pistol trained on his associates. 'Robbin' a few stagecoaches is all very well. Even the odd killin' I could handle. But this.' The sheer brutality made him pause for breath. 'Somewhere along the line, you've developed a vicious streak that's gonna get us all killed, Taggart. That's why I'm pullin' out.'

'I thought we were partners. Why have you changed?'

'It ain't me that's changed. You've become a mean-eyed killer. And I ain't runnin' with you or these lop-eared mules any longer.' Nolan backed out of the door still covering the other three.

Silvers eyed him coolly.

'If you feel that way,' he said, casually shrugging his slender frame. 'Then I won't stand in your way.'

Nolan gave a curt nod. 'Don't worry,' he assured Silvers, setting his hat straight. 'I won't tell nobody. Spike Nolan may be a gullible fool but he ain't no cat's-paw.'

'Good luck to you then, Spike.' The Kid's face remained blank, devoid of expression. He affected an innocent demeanour, outwardly accepting, if somewhat reluctantly, his ex-partner's withdrawal.

Spike holstered his gun, then walked down towards the edge of the trees where the horses had been tethered.

'Why did you let him go, boss?' queried Zeke with a puzzled frowned creasing his woolly chops.

Silvers just gazed ahead. A mystifying smile played across the young face.

Stepping back inside the cabin, he left the two brothers agog with bafflement. Seconds later he emerged clutching Crockett's Hawken rifle. Kneeling down, he laid the long barrel across the hitching rail and took careful aim.

Nolan had almost reached the pine cover when a deep boom split the air. Bouncing off the rock wall behind the cabin, the sharp crack echoed across the confines of the enclosed hollow.

The Kid's thin cruel lips drew back in a tight smile of satisfaction as Nolan slumped to the ground. The three men stared at the corpse for upwards of a minute. It did not move. Spike Nolan was dead.

Silvers tapped the barrel of the Hawken. His features bore a slanted look, almost of affection.

'A good long range weapon,' he remarked cordially. 'But give me the repeating action of a Henry any day.'

For the next three hours, until the evening sun lost its heat as it tipped beneath the scalloped western horizon, Kid Silvers had his sidekicks hunting around for the elusive gold-strike. When darkness at last forced them to call off the search, they made camp outside the cabin. There was no way any of them intended sleeping inside that mausoleum with its grizzly occupant.

'That paydirt has to be around here someplace,' spouted the Kid vehemently for the umpteeth time. 'Them nuggets is just a sample.'

'He could have dug 'em up at any number of sites within a day's ride,' opined Patch, prodding the carcass of a skinny rabbit he had shot. 'We could be here 'til dooms-day.' And he was not overly keen to spend another day with a corpse for company. 'I figure we should cut our losses and head back East,' he suggested, offering the Kid a slice of blackened meat. 'Hear tell there's been a big strike at Black Tail Gulch in South Dakota. A place called Deadwood.'

Silvers shrugged. He was not convinced. Absently chewing on the stringy repast, his devious mind churned over the perplexing conundrum. He was not about to be put off so easily. There was gold up here and he intended to find it.

On the following morning, with Patch Montana still urging a departure for pastures new, Silvers hit on the solution to the enigmatic gold-strike.

The flinty mask assumed a lurid tint.

'What's the first thing a prospector would do when he's struck a rich vein?' he said. The question, focused and coolly deliberate, was issued in a flat, calm voice. He didn't wait for a response. 'I tell you what I'd do. Get it registered perty damn quick, just to make things nice and legit.' The Kid aimed a toothy grin at his *amigos*. 'And that's what Crockett's done. All we gotta do now is find out which assay agent is holdin' the claim deeds.'

'That could be like lookin' for a needle in a hayrick,' replied Patch.

His brother nodded in agreement. 'Them fellers always keep a tight lid on that sort of information.'

Silvers shook his head, eyeing them with a mocking regard.

'That's why I'm the leader of this set-up, and you jerks take orders,' he scoffed, shaking his head. 'There's one person who'll know exactly which agent is holdin' the deeds.'

He held them with a frigid smile. It was Zeke who posed the right question.

'Who might that be then, boss?'

Silvers stayed his reply for effect, then said, 'Who else but Peg-Leg Carver. That bastard has had us doin' all his dirty work while he just sits back and waits for the goods to roll his way.' Now he'd figured out the problem, Silvers was becoming good and mad. 'The claim must be registered with that darned contact he was talkin' about. The jasper must have let it slip that a sizeable strike had been made on the Upper Yellowstone.'

'That's how Carver knew there was gold up here,' crowed an excited Patch Montana, quickly latching onto the Kid's zeal.

Zeke scratched his head. 'And the only guy livin' in this part of the country is Crockett.' The big hulk's turgid brain was slowly making headway.

'You guys sure catch on fast,' smirked the Kid. 'All we have to do now is exert some friendly persuasion on Carver to tell us where to find this contact of his.'

Zeke uttered a hoarse chortle.

Patch slapped his thigh in glee.

'We're gonna be rich after all, brother,' he howled in delight.

'Yahoo!' came back the animated response.

The two brothers leapt to their feet and danced a jig round the smouldering embers of the fire. Silvers took out a cigar and lit up.

'And now that Nolan is no longer in the picture, that means all the more loot for the three of us,' he drawled.

'Half for me, and half for you guys. OK?'

They nodded enthusiastically, continuing with their merry cavorting. Silvers gave a meaningful grunt, allowing himself the faintest trace of a smile.

TEN

A GRIM DISCOVERY

Having drawn a blank regarding his estranged brother, Link Taggart was heading up the Yellowstone for a final visit with Beartooth Crockett before returning to New Mexico. He wondered how the old trapper was faring. But first he had another visit to make. The detour along the north fork of the Huckleberry to see Marcy Waggoner was an extra half-day's ride to be savoured and relished. It could be months before he saw her again.

Smudger twisted her ears and gave a delighted whinny of approval. She was more than keen to become reacquainted with a certain paint stallion who had caught her eye on the previous visit.

Link threw a measured glance towards the early morning sun. Struggling over the eastern rim of the surging bluffs, the weak rays reflected off the icy caps of the topmost peaks. Flickering like the jewels in a crown, the sparkling mirage brought the whole of the valley to life. It was a sight to lift the most dejected spirit. But more important as far as Link was concerned, it brought the realization that he had enough time to spend a little with Marcy, and still make it to Crockett's cabin by sundown.

He nudged the chestnut mare along the side trail in the direction indicated by the painted sign that read *Wagon Wheel Trading Post*. So once again, the capricious tentacles of fate conspired to prevent the Taggart brothers meeting up.

A half-hour later, Kid Silvers passed the junction, heading south, but paid it no heed. Soon the three riders were emerging from the sepulchral confines of the pine-cloaked valley into open country dominated by spiny thorn and thick clumps of juniper. It was the Kid's intention to break off the main trail at the earliest opportunity.

'Why don't we just take the direct route through Moose Jaw?' enquired a puzzled Zeke Montana.

Silvers sighed wearily, spearing the big oaf with a condescending sneer.

'With two dead bodies behind us,' he said with slow deliberation, 'The last thing we want is to draw any unwelcome attention to ourselves. Folks have long memories out here in the wilderness. Like as not they'd remember three riders coming down from the Yellowstone. So the fewer people that see us the better.'

'We oughta have dumped the bodies in a ravine,' grumbled Patch. 'That way we'd have nothin' to worry over.'

Silvers knew he was right. Too late, the same notion had come into his own thoughts. He inwardly cursed himself for overlooking the obvious. But he was not about to admit that to anyone.

'So why didn't yuh do some'n about it?' he hollered, castigating the little guy with a bleak eye. 'Do I have to think of everythin' in this outfit?'

Both brothers hunched deeper into their saddles, suitably cowed.

They rode on in silence.

Unlike his more academically inclined brother, Corby Taggart had an eye for the terrain. Just by looking at how the land dipped, the creeks flowed, he could instinctively figure out the easiest and quickest route to follow.

It took them an extra half-day to reach Stackpole Draw where Peg-Leg Carver had his holding. But the Kid's wary attitude had paid off. They had not clapped eyes on another human soul. Only the prairie-dogs and circling buzzards had displayed any curiosity towards these biped intruders.

Approaching the shallow depression through which Stackpole Creek flowed, the trio slowed their mounts to a walk, dragging rein when Peg-Leg's dug-out hove into view. The old prospector had his back to them as they drew to a halt. Silvers eyeballed the bent form, an amused grimace cracking the otherwise cold demeanour.

Carver's attention was focused exclusively on the wooden rocker he was operating. As always, his thoughts were fixed on the life of ease and luxury he would once again enjoy when Silvers returned. With one hand pouring water over the gluey mixture of sand and gravel, he vigorously agitated the simple device with the other.

The idea was to separate any specks of gold that might be present in the tailings. It was one step up from the laborious drudgery of having to pan the creek-bed. Even so, it took a month of Sundays to make any headway. But for a lone prospector, this was the only method of sifting out the precious ore. And Carver had always been a loner.

That way he reckoned, you didn't have to share out the proceeds.

That was until Panhandle Pete McClintock let slip that a new discovery had been made on the Upper Yellowstone.

A dreamy smile drifted across the old guy's seamed contours. With any luck, he would be able to kiss this life goodbye if them three jackasses came up trumps. Visions of frothing champagne and the softest of feather beds floated before his wistful gaze.

Avidly scanning the riffles at the end of the rocker for tell-tale signs of paydirt, Carver only realized he had company when Silvers broke in on his cogitations.

'A guy could just walk right in here,' he scoffed, leaning on the saddle horn, 'club you down and snaffle that there poke.' He glanced across at his two sidekicks. 'That right, boys?'

The brothers nodded in unison.

Carver dropped the water-filled pannikin in total surprise and leapt to his feet. He peered around for his gun. It was way out of reach, leaning uselessly against the dug-out wall. His wiry frame trembled with fear. The leathery skin, cracked and ribbed like an old walnut, drew tight across the bony skull. Only when he finally recognized his partners did the sinewy features begin to relax.

He laughed at the Kid's notion, but the throaty rasp emerged more as a nervous cough.

'Not enough here to buy a decent meal,' he stressed forcefully whilst ensuring that the small bag was safely tucked away in his pocket. 'You fellers should have announced yer presence.' He snorted indignantly, tapping his scrawny chest. 'My poor old ticker's hammerin' fit to bust.'

Once he'd got his breath back, the old-timer was anxious to know if the gang's venture into the Upper Yellowstone had been a success. The grim regard staring back from the three faces told him that things had clearly not gone according to plan.

'Ain't yer got hold of the gold?'

The question drew no response save a brutal glower.

Silvers slid from the saddle. His boyish looks had set in a hard-baked crust, dark and sombre, brittle as frozen icicles. In a single movement, he closed the gap and grabbed the prospector's shirt hauling him up onto the tips of his toes.

'What do you think, old man?'

'But I know there's gold up in them hills. I just know it.'

'How d'yuh know?' hissed the Kid through tight lips. He choked off Carver's stuttering response. 'I'll tell yuh how. 'Cos that turkey you're big buddies with is holdin' the claim deeds.' He shook the old guy until his teeth rattled. 'Ain't that the truth. Spill it else I'll ring yer scrawny neck.'

'OK, OK!' squawked Carver, sucking in great lungfuls of air, 'Just give me a chance to get my breath and I'll tell yuh.'

Patch laid a placatory hand on the Kid's shoulder. 'Best to ease up on the old scrope,' he warned. 'else he'll keel over for sure.'

Silvers glowered at his partner but reluctantly took the hint.

'You got one minute to persuade me not to bury yuh right here,' he snapped.

Carver hurriedly made to reply, not wishing to waste a second of his allotted time.

'I allus figured the gold would be easy to find,' he crowed, nervously rubbing his gnarled hands together. 'I didn't say nothin' about the deeds figurin' you'd kinda persuade Crockett it was in his best interest to cough up the paydirt.'

'That jasper is one tough cookie,' drawled Zeke Montana with grudging respect.

Then Patch interjected with, 'Only trouble is, Nolan put his lights out for keeps afore we could make him talk.'

'I was wonderin' where that guy was,' remarked Carver.

It was Zeke who enlightened him. 'The boss didn't take kindly to that.' He sniggered mirthlessly. 'Terminated his contract with hot lead.'

His brother added for good measure. 'Great shot, eh, Kid?'

A cold ripple of fear crept down the old prospector's bent spine. Peering anxiously at the three sets of frigid peepers anchoring him to the spot, he realized his own intake of oxygen was hanging by a thread.

'Me and Panhandle Pete go back a spell. We used to get together and chew over the old days. He had the claim next to mine on the American back in the 'forty nine rush.' Carver's eyes misted over. 'Now that was some strike, boys, I tell yuh.'

'Get to the point, asshole,' snarled Silvers cutting off the oldster's reminiscences. He purposefully looked at his pocket watch. 'Yer time's almost run out.'

Carver swallowed hard. 'S-sure thing, Kid,' he stammered. 'One day last week Panhandle told me of this guy from the Upper Yellowstone who'd registered a big new strike.' Carver's eyes instinctively lit up at the mention of the discovery. 'Didn't mention no names. He'd been

116

sworn to secrecy. But drink allus loosens the most tight-lipped of *hombres*. And old Panhandle sure liked his moonshine. Next day he couldn't remember a durned thing. That's when I figured my luck had finally changed. Only trouble was this blamed leg.' He savagely banged the offending wooden limb. 'So you boys were the answer to my prayers.'

'Where is this jigger holed up?' rapped Silvers. 'And no smart-ass comments.'

'He has an office in Redemption.'

'Where's that?' enquired Patch.

'Small town on the far side of the Sugar Loaf,' replied Carver. 'About a day's ride west of here up Clark's Fork.'

'Then that's where we're headed.'

'What about me?' asked Carver rather nervously. 'We're still partners, ain't we?'

Silvers gave him a languid smile. He patted the old-timer playfully on the back. 'Sure we are, Peg-Leg,' he laughed adding with a conspiratorial wink aimed at his buddies. 'For now.'

Turning to Zeke, he said, 'You ride over to Moose Jaw and buy up all the gear we're gonna need for diggin' out this here gold.' His deceptively calm gaze then fastened on the prospector. 'Mr Carver here will write you out a list. The three of us are headin' for Redemption. Once we've gotten hold of the plans for Beartooth Creek, we'll meet you in the Last Chance saloon.'

'What's wrong with my stuff?' enquired Carver, feeling somewhat let down. 'I've been workin' this claim with it for nigh on three years.'

Silvers clicked his teeth derisively whilst gazing skywards.

117

'And look at it,' he snorted, aiming his toecap at the crumbling rocker box. 'This heap of junk is only fit for the rubbish dump.' He aimed a gob of spittle towards a rust-caked sifting pan. 'We need decent gear if the job's gonna be done properly.'

Carver shrugged, then went into the dug-out to prepare the list.

Ten minutes later they were ready to pull out.

The Kid fixed a mocking leer onto his silky-smooth features as Zeke went over to mount his horse.

'Ain't yuh forgettin' some'n?' he chided, not bothering to hide the derisory tone in his voice.

'Ugh?' Zeke looked up. His wide brow was furrowed in thought as the turgid brain cells slowly cranked up a notch.

Enjoying the big dude's confused discomfiture, Silvers waited. Then he asked, casually, 'How do you figure on payin' for all this propectin' paraphernalia, bozo?' Zeke's ugly puss wore a blank expression. He hadn't figured that one out. 'Surely you hadn't been intendin' to rob the bank. That would be breakin' the law.'

The others stood back enjoying the one-sided banter.

Eventually the Kid tired of the charade and let the fish off the hook. 'Catch this!' he rapped curtly, tossing over the small leather poke containing the five nuggets, adding brusquely, 'And don't lose it!'

Sarcasm was lost on Zeke Montana.

'Don't you worry none, boss,' he said, grateful to have been given some responsibility. 'I'll have the mule all loaded up and ready to go soon as you arrive.'

Silvers shook his head in bemusement as the big hulk gave a spirited wave before spurring off in the direction of Moose Jaw.

*

Link felt uneasy. But he couldn't figure out the cause. There was just something there, niggling at his craw.

He had almost reached the broad plateau and the edge of the treeline when he noticed Spike Nolan's blood-stained corpse. And the guy had been plugged in the back. As the sound of gunfire had not reached his ears, the indications pointed to the cowpoke's having being dead for some time. It also pointed to his brother having passed this way and got himself involved in some kind of lethal fracas.

So what had happened that led to a man being gunned down like this? It also seemed obvious that Beartooth Crockett had also been involved as they were so close to his cabin.

Link's gaze quickly shifted towards the cabin tucked away beneath the rocky overhang at the far side of the clearing. The atmosphere was thick with a premonition of doom. There was no sign of life. Even the normal chirruping of birds was absent. And the fact that no smoke could be seen drifting from the stone chimney was sufficient in itself to add to Link's growing sense of trepidation. Beartooth always kept a fire going. Even at the height of summer, nights on the Upper Yellowstone remained cold.

Drawing the Henry from its saddle boot, Link jacked in a load and cautiously nudged his mount towards the cabin. Smudger recoiled as a jackrabbit scooted from the undergrowth. An ominous precursor of things to come?

'Anybody home?' he called haltingly.

The summons went unanswered.

Now he knew that something was badly amiss. He took

a number of deep breaths to calm his frayed nerves. Gingerly stepping out of the saddle, his legs wobbled with foreboding. There was nobody around now, but Link was overly nervous of what he might discover inside the cabin.

'Can't just stand around admiring the view,' he murmured half to himself. The horse snickered in accord, wilfully nosing him forward.

'OK, old gal, I get the message,' came back the less than confident reaction as he approached the grim portal.

What he encountered on pushing open the door was like a scene from hell's inferno. It was as if a hurricane had swept through completely destroying everything in its wake. Not a single piece of furniture was intact. And the few cupboards there were had been emptied, the contents strewn about in wanton disorder.

Link's jaw trailed on the dirt floor. He stood in the doorway, transfixed by the horror of the odious tableau. Not to mention the smell. The cloying odour of death stung his nostrils.

So where was Beartooth?

Closer examination of the reckless destruction soon revealed the grim truth. A lurid trail of dried blood told its own gruesome tale.

Ogling the tortured cadaver of his erstwhile comrade, Link Taggart couldn't restrain a racking shriek of pure agony. He clutched at his writhing guts, the alien wail spewing forth in spasms of crazed anguish. Dragged up from deep within the bowels of his very being, the contents of his churning stomach soon followed. He retched violently until nought remained save a hollow ache.

Managing at last to stagger outside, he doused his burning face in the water butt in a futile attempt to somehow cleanse the execrable sight from his soul.

It was late in the afternoon, long shadows were angling across the broad clearing, before Link could gird himself to do what had to be done. In accordance with Jubal Crockett's wishes, he buried the trapper next to his beloved White Dove; both were now facing Heartbreak Falls. A beautiful locale for a finale, marred by such grievous memories. The spectacular cascade was sure living up to its mournful name.

After covering the grave with a layer of stones to deter predators, Link paused to say a few appropriate words. The platitudes of burial dispensed with, a cold resolve, hard as granite, imbued his bleak outlook.

He swore to bring the perpetrators of this heinous crime to justice, however long it might take. Slowly removing the revolver from the holster on his right hip, he spun the cylinder with explicit purpose.

'Somebody is going to pay dearly for what they've done to you, Beartooth.' The avowal was delivered in a flat monotone, devoid of expression, and all the more deadly as a consequence.

And if his brother was involved, too bad.

Before heading back down the valley, Link dug a shallow pit in which to inter Spike Nolan. Getting shot in the back appeared to indicate that the cowpoke had not been a willing party to the gruesome episode in the cabin.

As he pointed Smudger down the narrow trail, Link pondered on the sequence of events that had led him to this remote Wyoming valley, and a future that was manifestly uncertain.

ELEVEN

UNLUCKY FOR ZEKE

'Rider coming in!'

The announcement came from the blacksmith who had been making a set of branding-irons for a local ranch further up the valley. It was early morning and certainly not the time one would expect to receive a visit.

Marcy Waggoner forgot about her breakfast and hurried out onto the veranda. She screwed up her eyes to focus on the jogging form that was still a half-mile distant. Then, like the new sun pushing over the nearby peaks, recognition dawned.

'It's Link,' she called inside the house to her father. A vibrant smile matched the lustrous light in her emerald eyes. But just as quickly as it had arrived, the euphoria dissipated. Something wasn't right. Unlike the Link Taggart she had come to know and admire, this man exuded a tired aura of melancholy. His shoulders were slumped, the proud bearing despondent and subdued.

Brett Waggoner expressed the sombre query that was tugging at her own thoughts.

'What's young Taggert doing back here? I figured he'd be up around the Togwotee Pass by now.'

As the dejected horseman drew nearer, Marcy's sense of foreboding deepened appreciably.

'Something bad's happened,' she said, a worried frown darkening her satin features. 'I just know it.'

Without further comment, she ran across the flat dusty stretch fronting the trading post to meet the approaching rider. One look at his grim expression was enough to confirm her fears. Nothing was said. The girl restrained her natural inclination to ask questions. She sensed that Link would reveal the truth of the matter in his own good time. This was not the moment to press him.

Gently she took hold of Smudger's leathers and led the horse into the stable block, instructing the ostler to feed and water the animal. Then, linking arms with the hunched figure, she guided him towards the house, discreetly signalling for her father to give them some space.

The storeman nodded his understanding and withdrew.

Half an hour and three cups of strong black coffee later Link eventually spoke.

'Crockett's dead!' The brutal revelation emerged as a harsh retort, a cutting bite. 'He was tortured then shot.'

Slowly the horrific facts were revealed. Marcy posed an odd query here and there but in the main allowed Link to purge his soul uninterrupted. Following the distraught account, Marcy called for her father to join them.

'What are you going to do now?' he asked.

'Go after them, what else?' snapped Link as if there could be no other choice open to him.

'One man against hard-bitten critters like these?' replied Waggoner with a sceptical inflection. 'And you don't even know which way they went.'

'So what do you suggest?' rasped Link. 'That I just forget about it and go on home?'

'Pa's only being realistic, Link.'

'You need to report this to the sheriff at Jackson,' stressed the rancher. 'Scoby Chambers is a good man. He'll be able to organize a posse and get on their trail.'

'You're a lawyer, Link.' Marcy took hold of his hand. Her touch felt cool, a calming influence, something of which he was badly in need. And what more pleasing palliative could there be than the lovely Marcy Waggoner? 'Even if you do hunt these varmints down, they could just as easily kill you.' She peered deep into Link's tormented eyes, willing him to concede to her next suggestion. 'I'll come with you to Jackson. And together we'll make sure the law takes its rightful course. That's what you trained for all those years in Chicago, wasn't it?' He nodded realizing that what she said made sense as she added, 'So don't throw it all away on some hell-bent trail of vengeance.'

Once the next course of action had been agreed upon, Link was more than happy to enjoy a hearty breakfast before they set out together once again.

'You don't mind accompanying me to Jackson?' he asked while tucking in.

'Of course not,' came back the expected but no less welcome affirmation. Pausing to nudge Link's arm playfully, Marcy teased him with her own brand of whimsical humour. 'Can't have you getting yourself lost again, can I?'

'Guess not.' Link's response was rather diffident, his face assuming a markedly reddish hue.

The girl sensed his discomfort, hurrying on to forestall any further embarrassment.

'An army could lose itself among the maze of canyons and valleys in this part of the country. But I was born around here. Know the place inside out. Reckon I could find my way down to Jackson blindfolded. We'll need to pack enough victuals for three days. I trust you don't mind putting up with my cooking on the trail?'

Once again, Link mumbled rather haltingly. 'Seems like I'm already smitten. And it has nothing to do with the chow on offer.' The dark intensity of his gaze held the girl in a poignant embrace. Now it was Marcy's turn to feel abashed.

'I need to change into something more suitable,' came the flustered response as she turned away to hide her own awkwardness. 'And you need to see to the horses.' Then she quickly hustled out of the room.

Half an hour later she emerged from the house clad in a loose doeskin riding-skirt and green check shirt. Silky waves of auburn floated free beneath the beige Stetson. Her choice of apparel did nothing to conceal the seductive feminine contours. There was no mistaking the fact that Marcy Waggoner was all woman. Link could barely conceal a more than laudatory stare. It only served to affirm his budding affection for the girl.

'We pass through Moose Jaw on the way,' she said, unaware of the effect she was having on her ogling companion. 'It will give me the opportunity to drop off this outfit, which needs altering at the dressmaker's.'

Link muttered some garbled imprecation as they

spurred off down towards the banks of the Huckleberry. For some minutes they rode in silence as the grim task ahead reasserted its presence in their minds.

A flight of swallows shot past, following the course of the swirling river. Diving and twittering, at peace with their environment, the contrast with the austere expressions on the faces of the two travellers was manifest.

They arrived at the outskirts of Moose Jaw in the early afternoon. The recently installed clock atop the council offices chimed the hour of one.

Marcy arranged to meet Link one hour later.

With time to kill, he headed for the Last Chance saloon. He shouldered through the door, his eyes soon adjusting to the hazy gloom. Motes of dust floated in the beams cast by the harsh sunlight. Business was slow. Only two other people were present, and one of those was the small portly jasper tending bar.

Link's gaze automatically focused on the other fellow. He was hunched over a drink, his face in shadow. Link stepped up to the bar and ordered a beer. Accepting the drink, he sunk half the cooling liquid in a single draught.

'A mighty hot day,' he commented.

'Sure is,' replied the drinker, turning to face the newcomer. He was a burly critter, hard-nosed and unkempt, sporting a bushy black beard. The grey hat covering a straggle of greasy hair was sweat-stained and frayed at the edges. 'Only greenhorns or mad dogs stay out in this heat.'

Link nodded in agreement, raising his beer glass to finish the contents. It never reached his open mouth. His eyes, fascinated, were fixed upon the big guy. The forthright stare was both obvious and disconcerting. Not to mention down right intrusive.

The man couldn't help but notice.

'Somethin' wrong, mister?'

Silence.

'I asked yuh what was wrong,' rasped the hulk, drawing himself off the bar. 'Do I know yuh?' His tone had hardened, assuming a stony challenge.

Link's visible shock at seeing Jubal Crockett's prized circlet of teeth gracing the bull neck of this polecat soon passed. He stepped back a pace, facing the guy. His mouth suddenly felt dry.

In a low voice oozing menace and anguish in equal measure, his finger jabbed at the all-important item.

'Where did you get that?' he croaked.

'What yuh on about?'

'The necklace. Who gave it to you?'

The guy's mallet of a paw fingered the toothy collar.

'What's it to you?'

Link eyes narrowed to thin slits. He sucked in a deep gulp of air.

'I'll ask you one more time,' he rasped, squaring off his shoulders, tension rippling through his taut frame. 'And if I don't get the right answer, you're dead meat.'

Even a slow-witted hulk like Zeke Montana now realized it had been a mistake to appropriate the bear-tooth necklace. It had seemed such a fine piece of adornment at the time. Something with which to impress the ladies. Now he wasn't so sure. This guy clearly knew the trapper and suspected foul play.

Zeke did the only thing his obtuse brain could work out under the circumstances. He went for his gun. Slow-witted he may have been in mind, but his physical reflexes more than compensated. Unlike the tales he would have fabricated regarding the origin of the necklace, the six notches on his .36 double-action Cooper revolver were for real.

Unfortunately, he was too close to his opponent. Effective gunplay was best undertaken at a distance. And Link was no slouch himself. As soon as Montana's hand dropped, he flung the remaining dregs of beer into the hulk's repellent kisser. It was enough to slow him down. He staggered back, shaking the drops from his face.

Link took full advantage of the bruiser's hesitancy to sink a hefty right into his bulging stomach, followed by two solid jabs to the exposed chin. The guy backfooted along the bar. Before Montana could regain the initiative, Link drew his own pistol and slammed it butt-end across the guy's head.

That was enough. Montana uttered a throaty grunt and slumped to the floor, out cold.

But Link still hadn't got any answers. Quickly he ran outside and unhooked his lariat. In no time, the comatose tough was tied up and leaning against the wall.

'Give me a pitcher of water,' Link snapped at the cowering barkeep.

The sweating beer-puller continued to stare open-mouthed.

Link slammed the pistol loudly on the bar. 'A jug of water, *now!*' he barked.

'S-sure, m-mister,' stammered the 'keep, hurriedly sliding a glass jug along the shiny bar top. 'Anything you say.'

Link grabbed up the jug and flung the contents into the bearded mush. It had the desired effect. Burbling and groaning, the bruiser surfaced. Trying to rise, he suddenly realized his predicament.

'What in tarnation is this?' he howled, struggling ineffectually against his bonds.

'You haven't answered my question.' A hard-edged rap blasted into Zeke Montana's right ear. 'So I'll ask it again. And this time if I don't get the right answer, the job will be finished ... permanently.' He drew the Whitney and hauled back the hammer to full cock. The cold steel of the barrel jammed into the guy's ear. 'Where did you get the necklace?'

Zeke knew then that he was kiboshed. And the gruesome details emerged in a torrent. He was, however, anxious to point out to his captor that he had only been a bystander, forced into taking part by their brutal leader.

'And did this pesky varmint have a name?' enquired Link.

'He went under the handle of Kid Silvers on account of the conchos he wore on his vest and hat. But his real name was Taggart.'

'Corby!' The single word hissed out in a staccato burst of acrimony moderated only by a hint of disbelief. Could his own brother really be involved in murder? He always knew the kid was rebellious, aggrieved by Link's own success. But surely he wouldn't have resorted to such abhorrent means to assuage his bitterness.

'You sure the kid's real name is Corby Taggart?' he pressed the stunned captive.

'No doubts on that score,' answered Montana. 'My brother Patch let it slip once and gotten hisself a right mouthful. The Kid don't like bein' reminded of his past.' Zeke shook the muzziness from his lethargic brain. 'You acquainted with the Kid then, mister?'

'You could say that.'

Zeke waited for him to elaborate. But Link remained tight-lipped, staring vaguely into the opaque void of his past.

'What yuh gonna do with me?'

The nervous enquiry dragged Link's mind back to the here and now as he addressed the stunned bartender. 'Is there a lock-up in this town?'

'Two blocks down on the right. You can't miss it. It's the only stone building in Moose Jaw.'

'Help me get this polecat outside.'

The barman hurried round to raise the still groggy bulk of Zeke Montana off the floor. He was only too pleased to see the backs of both of them.

Once on the boardwalk, Link jabbed his revolver into Zeke's back urging him down the street in the direction indicated by the barman.

Strolling casually towards him on the opposite side was Marcy. She drew to a halt on witnessing the strange procession. The staggering form of a hulking bruiser was followed by Link and a fluttery little man. A pair of curious hounds brought up the rear, vainly hoping for some choice titbit to come their way. She crossed the street, quickening her pace, to join them.

'What happened?' she queried.

'I'll tell you everything on the trail to Redemption,' he replied without breaking his stride.

'Redemption?' came back the startled retort. 'Why are we going there?'

'Just open the door of this here lock-up,' he replied curtly. Marcy held her peace, sensing that this was not the moment for protracted explanations.

The square sandstone blockhouse was set back in its

own yard surrounded by a chain-link fence. It stood out like a red carbuncle emblazoned with a hand-painted sign that read: *Moose Jaw Hoosegow. Lock up before you leave.* A printed instruction sheet pinned to the solid oak door finished with: *Emptied by Scoby Chambers, County Sheriff, once a month. Key available from the Council Offices.*

There being no other occupants, the heavy brass key was stuck in the lock.

Zeke Montana was unceremoniously pushed into the tiny one-roomed prison cell and the door firmly shut and locked behind him. The only light came from a tiny barred window high up on one wall.

Link's next remark was to the hovering barkeep who was anxious to be shot of this unwholesome affair and return to the more genteel pastime of beer-pulling.

'When is the county sheriff due next?'

The little man considered the question by scratching his bald pate.

'Another two weeks at least,' he said.

Link passed him the large key.

'Hand this in to the council office sometime.' Without further comment he led Marcy away from the lock-up towards their tethered horses. They mounted up and headed north out of town leaving the flustering barman to inform the town council that they had a prisoner to feed.

Nothing more was said until they had left Moose Jaw far behind and were heading up a shallow gradient flanked by stands of ponderosa pine. Only then did Link break the tense silence revealing the mind-blowing encounter with Zeke Montana and the discovery that his brother had become a hard-bitten outlaw going under the handle of Kid Silvers.

The rest of the grisly details followed in series of brief spurts, punched out as Link felt himself able to cope with the bizarre sequence of events. It was hard to come to terms with the realization that his brother, his own flesh and blood, was a cold-blooded killer, instrumental in the sickening demise of Beartooth Crockett, the man who had befriended him. Clancy Balloo had doubtless gone the same way.

Link could only guess how many others had ended up as notches etched onto Corby's gun butt.

'Shouldn't we be telling the sheriff all this?' Marcy had waited until the whole sorry episode had unfolded before venturing to make the tentative suggestion.

'That would take too long now we know what the gang's intentions are.' His eyes misted over. 'And now I know for sure that Corby is involved, it's up to me to see this thing through to the bitter end. I don't have any choice in the matter.' He hauled Smudger to a halt turning to face this girl who, he now realized, was the only one for him. 'You go back,' he said, holding her hand. 'There's likely to be lead flying and I don't want you getting hurt in the crossfire.'

She fixed him with a stubborn gleam, her slim figure stiff and erect.

'You know the way to Redemption then?'

'Well no, but—'

'No buts. You'd only get yourself lost again.'

'But this could be dangerous.'

'I said no buts. If you intend going after them you need a guide. And I'm the only one available.' She smiled, her oval face lighting up. The radiant glow shone through the dull verdure of the forest. 'So that's an end of it. You're stuck with me.'

132

He met her sunny expression with a look that spelt more than mere appreciation. Link knew now that he was falling deeply in love with this vision from heaven.

'When this is over,' he murmured rather bashfully, 'I'd like to feel we can become maybe more than just good friends. What d'you think?'

A coquettish twinkle playing across the silky features faded as the pragmatic side of her nature reasserted itself.

'We'll see,' was all the encouragement he was going to receive at this stage. There was still the matter of bringing Kid Silvers to justice. 'As things stand, just be thankful that all of us Waggoners are taught to be crack shots from the moment we can hold a rifle.' She thumped him playfully in the chest. 'And that includes the women.'

With that incisive comment, she spurred ahead, leaving Link to ponder on whether his advances had been spurned, or just put onto the back burner. You never could tell where women were concerned.

TWELVE

REDEMPTION

Peg-Leg Carver was in the lead. He was the only one of the three horsemen who knew the way to Redemption. Riding in single file, it had taken the better part of the day to pick their way through the dense covering of trees that marked the lower reaches of the tributary valley known as Clark's Fork.

Beyond Wolverine Lake, the gradient had become steadily more acute, slowing their pace considerably. On the steeper sections, where chaotic heaps of loose boulders posed a definite hazard to life and limb, they were forced to discard the dubious comfort of the saddle and walk. All except Carver, the only one riding a mule, who took the opportunity to moan that his injured appendage was paining him rotten. This riled the Kid who was finding the going extremely tough. He was becoming ever more exasperated.

'How much further?' he barked at Carver for the third time.

The old prospector grunted, but this time was able to

offer a positive response. He pointed a gloved finger to a rounded pinnacle of grey limestone thumbing the blue sky ahead. A lone buzzard gracefully circled the squat landmark. It was the only creature they had spotted since leaving a herd of mountain goats grazing beside the placid waters of Wolverine Lake.

'That's the Sugar Loaf,' he observed. 'Redemption is on the far side.'

'About time,' rasped the Kid. Like all Westerners, he detested being cast afoot.

Cresting the rise adjacent to the soaring landmark, the two men were once again able to mount up. On the far side of the pass, the ground fell away to reveal a wide amphitheatre with a disparate cluster of shacks and grey tents holding centre stage.

All around, tree-stumps poked out from the bare earth, the wood having been commandeered for building and mining purposes. It was clear that Redemption was of recent origin, a boom town in the throes of exploiting a new gold-strike. All across the wide bottomland, heaps of ore-bearing gravel had turned this once serene locale into an immense labour camp. Barely a leaf or a blade of grass could be seen amidst the bleak wasteland. This was the sharp edge of hard-rock mining and no place for the faint-hearted.

Only time would tell whether the new settlement prospered and set down permanent roots, or died an ignominious death similar to a thousand others that littered the Western frontier.

All that interested Silvers, however, was locating the assay office and getting hold of that all-important map of Beartooth Creek.

Redemption was barely more than a clutter of ugly hutments huddling along the single main street. Not a lick of paint was in evidence to relieve the barren greyness of the scene. The three riders hauled rein at the western limit, surveying their bleak surroundings with jaundiced eyes.

'So where do we find this assay agent?' voiced Silvers impatiently.

'He lives in a cabin on the far side of town up a side-draw,' replied Carver, nudging his mount forward.

'Hold it!' rapped the Kid. 'Any chance of getting out there without being spotted? The fewer jiggers that eyeball us the better.'

'We could take the high trail above town. It's longer but we ain't likely to meet up with anyone.'

'Then that's what we'll do.'

Carver shrugged, then heaved on the reins, leading them across a stark desert littered with the abandoned detritus of failed or exhausted mining claims. Soon they were climbing above the grim jumble of buildings along a thin game-trail.

It was another half-hour before they dropped down through stands of flaking juniper and cottonwood into a shallow draw. At the end stood an isolated log cabin. A light burned in the single window.

'There it is!' hollered Carver.

'I figured that,' spat Silvers acidly. 'And keep yer voice down. We don't want this jasper knowin' there are three of us.'

After they had tethered their mounts behind a rocky bluff, Silvers studied the cabin. Coal-black eyes squinted, trying to latch on to any movement. His nerves were strung tight as banjo-strings now that the crunch time had arrived.

He forced his voice to remain cool and dispassionate. His first comment was aimed at the prospector.

'Make out this is just a social call.' The whisper emerged as a throaty rasp. He coughed to hide the hesitancy. 'We'll be outside the door listenin'. Soon as you've gotten him to admit the title deeds are in the cabin, we'll bust in and take over.'

'You won't kill him, will yuh, Kid?' It was more a plea than a question.

Silvers drew his revolver and jabbed the old guy ominously in the belly.

'Just make sure you do the business,' he hissed, 'And leave the rest to me and Patch. Now beat it!' Unceremoniously, he pushed Carver out into the open. As soon as the old dude had entered the cabin, the two desperadoes hurried across to press themselves flat against the rough log walls, ears attuned to the conversation being conducted within.

When Carver hobbled into the assay office, Panhandle Pete McClintock was checking a sample of ore. A small magnifying-glass was screwed into his right eye. On his left stood a set of weighing-scales.

He was a small ruddy-faced dude in his mid-forties with heavy jowls concealing a bull neck. Round and portly, he had clearly gone to seed since abandoning the tough job of placer mining for the more lucrative and infinitely easier life of an assay agent.

'Nice to see yuh, Peg-Leg,' he warbled cheerily, setting down the chemical analysis tube he had been using. 'Ain't seen yuh since that last blow-out we had in Moose Jaw. So what brings you up here?' A high-pitched squeak meant to be a laugh issued from between thick rubbery lips. 'Not made a big strike, have yuh?' The friendly joshing implied that McClintock had little faith in his *compadre's* striking it rich from his present claim.

'Just came up for the fishin',' replied Carver somewhat unconvincingly.

'Only good fishin' round here is for gold,' came back the acerbic quip from Panhandle. 'And there ain't no more claims left worth the buyin'.' He passed over a jug of moonshine. 'Help yerself,' he offered. 'It's just been brewed.'

Carver tipped the jug to his lips and took a deep snort. He needed it. He could almost feel Kid Silver's frosty gaze boring into his back.

'Talkin' about claims,' he began rather diffidently. 'Was that true what you said about there bein' gold on the Upper Yellowstone along Beartooth Creek?'

Panhandle Pete shot him a look laced with suspicion. He set down the eyeglass.

'How do you know about that?' The challenge was blunt and to the point. 'Any talk of particular claims is confidential information.'

Carver hurried on, anxious to get his part in this charade over and done with.

'You let it slip after polishin' off that second jug at my place. Don't you remember?' Carver tried to stay calm, keeping the edginess at bay. He failed.

'So what's this all about? Are you anglin' to get in on the action?' The assay agent's voice had taken on a measured hardness. 'Well you can go to hell. That was a mistake. I ought never to have mentioned it to you, nor anyone else. If'n I went around divulgin' all my clients' business, I'd soon end up in the mortuary with lead poisonin'.'

138

That was the moment Silvers chose to enter the fray.

Bursting open the door, he shouldered in, the Remington cocked and raised.

'You'll be eatin' a lead sandwich sooner than you expected, mister, if'n you don't hand over them deeds.'

'And maybe I'll add a slice or two off that fat hide of your'n for good measure,' added Patch Montana, brandishing the large Bowie in one hand and a double-gauge Loomis in the other.

'You treacherous skunk!'

McClintock's snarled retort was aimed at his so-called buddy. At the same time, he lunged for the shooter he always kept under the counter.

That was his final utterance. He didn't stand a chance. A deafening blast rent the static air. Flame erupted from both barrels of the shotgun as they punched a hole the size of a derby hat in his stomach. The force of the lethal blast slammed Panhandle back against the wall of the cabin.

Thick gouts of choking white smoke filled the small room. Silvers coughed as the stench of burnt powder clogged his nostrils.

Carver groaned aloud as he staggered over to a chair and sat down. This wasn't how things were supposed to have panned out, so to speak. He had figured Panhandle would have huffed some, then come round to their way of thinking for a cut of the proceeds. Now the guy was gravefodder.

Silvers cut through his maudlin recriminations.

'He must have all the deeds stashed away in that tin box.' He pointed to a rusty filing cabinet in the corner. 'Use that Loomis to blow it open, Patch.'

Montana nodded, cracking open the lethal weapon. Slipping two new cartridges into the barrel, he stepped behind the counter and pointed the gun at the heavy lock. Another ear-splitting blast shook the cabin. Wafting the smoke aside, Montana yipped with glee. 'Just like peelin' open a tin of peaches,' he cried enthusiastically, like a young kid on Christmas Day.

Silvers elbowed his confederate aside, quickly delving amongst the array of papers. Nimble fmgers feverishly searched through the various files. Within minutes the cabin was white with superfluous paper.

Then he found what he was looking for.

A hungry glint in his eyes matched the lurid smile that registered pure greed. Avidly scanning the hand-drawn map of Beartooth Creek, he prodded a finger at the location where the gold had been discovered.

'It's no more than a half-mile west of the cabin,' he purred excitedly, 'But without this map, it would have taken months, even years to find it.' Then his gaze fastened onto the assay report. 'It says here that the ore sample he brought in is Grade A.'

'What does that mean, Kid?' enquired an equally ecstatic Patch Montana.

'It means that we're gonna be rich.'

'Don't forget our deal,' whined Carver from across the room. 'There would have been no map without my help.'

Silvers squared off to face the old-timer. No words passed his thin lips, but the hard-bitten stare made Carver's blood turn to ice. His gaunt features turned white as he cowered back in fear. Slowly the Kid lifted the Remington. His thumb raked back the hammer. Carver's mouth opened, but total horror froze his voice-box solid.

Only a rough croak emerged.

'You ain't no use to me any more, Peg-Leg,' Silvers murmured nonchalantly. 'And that deal. You got it in writing?' His finger tightened on the trigger.

It was Patch who saved the old prospector's bacon.

'We still need him, boss,' he urged. 'Who else knows about diggin' out the gold?'

The Kid hesitated. His partner was right. Neither of them was a gold miner. And Zeke didn't know one end of a shovel from the other. He eased the hammer back.

'Seems like your time on this earth ain't over just yet,' crowed Silvers.

Carver's thin shoulders slumped as he sighed with relief. But he knew that once the gold had been extracted, he would be surplus to requirements. At some point in between, he would have to make his move.

Before they left the assay office, Silvers made certain that Panhandle Pete would not be found. Patch and Carver carried the body outside and tipped it down the well. The assay agent would be missed, but nobody would have an inkling for some time as to his whereabouts.

Within an hour of arriving in Redemption, the outlaws were heading back down the trail to Moose Jaw. They had met no one. All they had to do now was collect Zeke and head back to Beartooth Creek. Within a month they would all be wallowing in riches beyond their wildest dreams. All courtesy of Mister Jubal Crockett.

But nothing ever runs that smoothly.

On the upgrade just below the Sugar Loaf, Patch Montana complained that his horse had a loose shoe.

'He's been limping for the last mile. If I don't rest him, the old guy'll give out on me for sure.'

141

'What yuh gonna do about it?' rapped Silvers, displaying obvious irritation. Any hold-ups now were the last thing he needed.

'You push on ahead,' Patch suggested. 'I'll tighten the shoe as best I can then catch you up. I can get it fixed properly in Moose Jaw.'

Silvers muttered a few disobliging oaths, then said curtly, 'We'll make camp beside Wolverine Lake.' Then without another word, he nodded for Carver to lead off.

THIRTEEN

BLACK TOP MESA

'Redemption is on the far side of that cone of rock up ahead,' commented Marcy, pointing to a domed upthrust of limestone crowned with an icy canopy. It was planted on the left flank of a broad ledge known locally as Black Top Mesa.

Link smiled.

'The Sugar Loaf,' he remarked with a trace of awe in his voice. 'Never figured I'd be passing it on a man-hunt like this.' The girl eyed him quizzically as he explained. 'An old jasper back in Thermopolis told me to head straight for it once I'd got over Togwotee Pass. Said I couldn't go wrong.' He laughed out loud, repeating the vague instruction with an ironic click of the tongue. It all seemed so long ago. And so much had happened in the meantime. 'Couldn't go wrong. Truth of the matter is that since then, nothing has gone right.' Then he remembered who was guiding him. The hang-dog expression vanished in an instant. 'Excepting, of course, meeting up with you.'

Marcy acknowledged the compliment with a modest

143

nod. But ever the pragmatist, she drew his wavering attention back to the sombre task in hand.

That of locating Link's brother and bringing him to justice.

For much of the next hour they were forced to lead the horses up the rough trail before eventually cresting the lip onto the flat-topped mesa. Stunted clumps of juniper and dwarf oak flourished amidst the untidy clutter of rocks. And on their left rose the regal splendour of the Sugar Loaf, its cliff face striated with cracks and fissures unseen by the naked eye from a distance.

The mesa was less than 200 yards across before the trail descended steeply. Link nudged his horse towards the far side. The two riders paused on the lip of the north face at the point where the trail suddenly made an abrupt swing round a tight corner.

Marcy informed her companion that a dangerous section lay around the bend that required extreme care and concentration. Link nodded his understanding. The grim recollection of Beartooth Crockett's untimely demise once again reared its ugly head to haunt his memories.

Allowing the mounts to choose their own pace, Marcy led the way forward. They had just tightened the reins in preparation for the loose descent of the fractured north face when Marcy signalled an abrupt halt.

'What is it?' asked Link, taken by surprise.

Marcy put a finger to her pursed lips, indicating silence.

She pointed down towards a clump of mountain-ash hugging the stony trail that followed a precarious twist up the brutally riven face of the mesa. At first Link could see nothing. Narrowed eyes squinted hard, following the girl's urgent pointing. The first intimation that they were not

144

alone was a tumble of dislodged pebbles and dust trickling over the edge of the trail into the dark abyss below.

Then he saw the crown of a battered old hat. The face of the owner was concealed beneath the wide brim, his searching gaze concentrated solely on picking a safe course with his mule on a loose rein. He was a small fellow, rather skinny, unlike his tall partner who was on foot and leading a mottled grey gelding.

Link drew in a sharp intake of breath. A shudder tugged at his backbone. He recognized that horse and knew it would have a Box T branded stamped onto its rump. Spears of light glinted off the guy's hat – conchos. Even at that distance, Link knew that he was about to come face to face with his estranged brother.

Or Kid Silvers as he was now called.

So intent were the two desperadoes on negotiating the tricky ascent that they failed to notice the other two riders about to descend the trail from above.

Spurred on by a desperation to avoid being spotted, Link quickly backed Smudger up, praying that no stones would be dislodged to warn those below. The chestnut had quickly latched on to her master's edginess and made no mistakes. Marcy quickly followed. Stepping down from their saddles, they hurriedly pulled their mounts behind a cluster of boulders.

Link checked his revolver, sliding in a sixth cartridge to give it a full load. Marcy drew her Winchester and levered a shell into the breech.

Then they settled down behind a large rock close to the where the trail emerged onto the mesa top. About ten minutes later their finely tuned hearing picked up the muffled sound of shod hoofs scraping on rock.

Link's nerves were at fever-pitch. Knuckles, blanched white as snow, clutched the butt of his revolver. Marcy appeared much calmer, her manner brisk. Red lips opened slightly to reveal tight-clenched teeth as she rested a smooth cheek against the rifle's rosewood stock.

The waiting was almost over. Time hung heavy across the parched aridity of Black Top Mesa.

A lizard scooted across Link's right boot. It paused, flashing a fearful look around its arid surroundings before disappearing into a hole. The tiny creature, sensing that a violent confrontation was imminent, was clearly anxious to seek cover. Overhead, the inevitable predators were gathering. Buzzards always seemed to know when trouble was brewing with a deluxe feast in the offing.

Link scowled, then stroked back the revolver's hammer to half-cock. He had no intention of being on the menu. But he faced a bewildering situation. All the evidence pointed to his brother's having turned into a ruthless outlaw capable of snuffing out a human life without compunction. On the other hand, he couldn't quite believe that his own kin could have allowed himself to sink so low.

And it need never have come to this. The whole purpose of his trip to Wyoming had been to inform Corby that the storekeeper he had gunned down was going to make a full recovery. If his brother really had the stain of blood on his hands then there was no going back.

But he had to know for sure.

That was when their quarry arrived.

First, the pitted crown appeared followed by its owner. Link noticed that the wearer was a grizzled old jigger, not the sort he would have expected Corby to consort with.

146

Unhooking a water-bottle from the pommel of his saddle, the old guy unscrewed the stopper and took a few sips.

Kid Silvers followed behind, his shoulders slumped.

'Give me that!' he snapped, grabbing the bottle. His black conchoed hat, dusty and sweat-stained, hung down his back. The taxing ascent had taken its toll. His breath jerked out in short wheezing bursts. He untied a grubby bandanna from around his neck and wiped the sweat from a dirt-encrusted brow.

'This better be worth it,' he grumbled, aiming a twisted scowl at his ageing partner. The Kid tipped the remaining contents of the bottle down his parched throat.

'Don't drink so fast,' cautioned the wizened little fellow.

But it was too late. The warm liquid headed down the wrong channel almost choking the young hardcase. Retching hacks elicited a wry smile from the seamed visage of the oldster, which he struggled to conceal.

That brief distraction was the moment for which Link had been waiting.

He leapt out from his place of concealment and challenged the two brigands.

'Raise your hands,' he yelled, brandishing his pistol, 'and step away from those mounts.'

The two outlaws swung to face this startling encounter. Shock registered on both their faces. This was the last thing they had expected. Both were stunned into immobility.

Silvers was the first to recover. But only to blurt out a single rap on recognizing his antagonist.

'Link!' he exclaimed, 'Where d'you spring from?'

'Just keep your mits where I can see them,' snapped Link. 'Then we'll talk.'

Although surprised, Peg-Leg Carver was not dismayed, unlike his youthful partner. 'You and this jigger acquainted?' he asked. A hint of shrewd cunning reflected in the lift of the old prospector's skinny shoulders. This sudden change in their circumstances could work in his favour.

'More than acquainted, mister,' replied Link, maintaining a steady gun hand. 'This guy you've thrown in with happens to be my brother.'

'Your brother!' Now it was Carver's turned to be nonplussed. 'So how come you're holdin' a gun on him?'

Link's reply was aimed at his brother.

'I came out here to tell you that Hardrock Forester is going to make a full recovery. Pa asked me to bring you back to Cimarron.'

The Kid's mouth dropped open at this revelation.

'So I needn't have skipped town after all? Is that what you're a-tellin' me?'

'You would have had to stand trial. But with a good lawyer—'

'I presume that means you,' interjected Corby acidly.

'Sure it does. With me on the podium, you would have been looking at a substantially reduced sentence.'

'So what are we talkin' about?'

'It *would* have been three years. And you *could* have been out in two with good behaviour.' Link stared hard at his brother. His next remark was the one he had been dreading. His voice sounded hoarse, croaky, as if it belonged to someone else. 'But it's too late for all that now, isn't it? You've gone too far down the wrong trail. Carrying on like this is only going to earn you a one-way trip to the gallows.'

'What yuh gonna do about it then . . . big brother?'

The Kid was fast recovering his composure.

'Are you telling me that all these things I've been hearing about are all true?'

'What's that, then?'

'That you've become a thief and a cold-blooded killer?'

Corby gave a devil-may-care shrug.

'The truth, the whole truth and nothing but the truth, Mister Lawyerman.' He held up his right hand mockingly. 'So help me God.' Then he aimed a venomous look at his brother, accompanying it with a savage cut: 'But you'll never take me in. Never, I tell yuh. There's no way I'm goin' back to Cimarron only to end up as gallows-fodder with you and Pa soundin' off about what a disappointment I was to the family.' He spat in the dust.

But the ranting diatribe was all a ruse. Turning side on, he allowed the hand on his blind side to fall gradually. He was a lot faster than his brother where gunplay was involved. Another couple of inches and he would dive to the left and slap leather.

But Marcy Waggoner had noticed the surreptitious move.

'Keep them mitts grabbing air, mister,' she urged, injecting an element of vehemence into the blunt command. The thrusting Winchester lent added emphasis to the girl's aggressive stance. 'And don't figure 'cos I'm a woman that this rifle is just for show.'

The Kid scoffed but it was an empty gesture. Marcy had confidently made her point. His arms lifted, if somewhat reluctantly to rejoin those of his partner.

FOURTEEN

STAND OFF

Patch Montana eyed the backs of his partners dolefully from beneath thick shaggy eyebrows as they disappeared along the trail. Then he scowled at the offending shoe now almost hanging off his bronc's front hoof. There was no way he could mount up with it in that condition. Another half-mile and the nag would certainly have gone lame, maybe even stumbled and broken a leg. Being cast afoot in this outlandish terrain, he would like as not end up as a tasty treat for some wandering scavenger.

Patch nervously looked around him. Only a couple of desert rats peered back from under the sheltering canopy of a prickly pear.

At least the nails were still in evidence. All he needed was to hammer them back into place. Just so long as the beast was not required to do anything more than walk, he should make it back to Moose Jaw.

A handy rock would have to suffice as a hammer.

Half an hour later, he was back in the saddle. Carver and the Kid would be forced to walk up the narrow trail

150

below Black Top Mesa. Maybe he could catch them up on the down-grade beyond.

Nearing the Sugar Loaf, the distinctive landmark appeared to take on a life all its own, winking at him as the light reflected off its frosty coat. And with the sun at its zenith, Patch was sweating bucketfuls. Like his *compadres* before him, his whole attention was focused on safely gaining the plateau. So it came as a pleasant relief when he reached the sharp bend on the mesa's scalloped rim.

That was when he heard voices.

Could his ears be playing him tricks? Pausing, he concentrated hard. There it was again. Definitely voices, and coming from just around the bend on the mesa top. Not only that but one of them appeared to be female. This didn't make sense. There was only way to find out the truth.

Patch ground-hitched the woebegone cayuse and climbed up a narrow fissure to one side of the trail. The brief scramble brought him out on a ledge above the parley that was taking place on the far side. Careful not make any noise, he knelt down and bellied across the grey heat of the rocky shelf before cautiously raising his head. Only at the last moment did he remember to remove his high-crowned Texas sombrero.

A low whistle issued from between puckered lips. Some dude and his gal had got the drop on the Kid and that crazy prospector.

Did that mean the law was onto them for that killing on the Upper Yellowstone? Or was it any number of other capers with which they had been involved? And what of his brother Zeke, where did he fit into the puzzle?

This and a heap of other niggling conundrums would have to wait.

Scuttling crablike back down off the shelf, he edged round the far side of the large rocky ledge to emerge on the flats below. A wolfish smile revealed broken teeth stained yellow from too much baccy-chewing.

Silvers was the first to spot his arrival. His taut features remained deadpan, inscrutable. Only a slight tightness around the eyes betrayed him. Not even his brother noticed, so intent was Link on castigating his younger kin.

'Drop them hoglegs. And don't make no sudden moves.'

The blunt command lanced through the tense atmosphere. Link froze. Marcy turned and uttered a fearful cry.

'Do it, mister,' came the repeated summons, this time spiked with a mordant edge. 'And you as well, girly, unless you wanna taste lead.'

The pair realized they had no choice but to obey. The guns thudded on the hard rock of the mesa.

'That's better,' smirked Patch, easing his shooter to half-cock. 'Now move away from them irons.'

The Kid let slip a giggle of pure relief.

'What kept yuh, Patch?' he burbled, lowering his arms. Carver was less than enthusiastic about Montana's untimely intervention.

The Kid's next remark drained the blood from the prospector's raddled visage as Silvers' hand strayed towards the revolver on his right hip. The intention to liquidate the evidence standing between him and freedom was indelibly scrawled across the surly countenance.

'It woulda been better for the both of us if you had never come after me, big brother,' snarled Silvers. Patch's thick eyebrows curled upwards at this unexpected revelation. 'Now you've gone and forced my hand,' continued Silvers in a flat, even tone. His fingers tapped the gun butt.

Had he bothered to heed the old prospector's tense and apprehensive countenance he could have prevented what was about to be played out on the dark mesa top.

Carver knew he had to act. Lives were at stake, not least his own. The lifeline that had so recently been tossed his way was about to be irrevocably severed. The ageing visage was a twitching mass of leathery wrinkles. He threw a panic-stricken look towards his two 'partners'. Both were gazing fixedly at their adversaries.

It was now or never, before the Kid made his draw.

Take out Montana first because his gun was already drawn, then the Kid.

Before he realized it, the old Dragoon was in his hand. Still they didn't suspect. He prayed that the loose ratchet wheel would hold. He'd been meaning to have it repaired by the gunsmith in Moose Jaw. Now it was too late.

Hauling back the hammer, the sharp double-click sounded brutally loud. Momentarily, time stood still on Black Top Mesa. Then the old gun bucked twice, spitting orange flame and hot lead.

The first shot punched a hole in Montana's shoulder. It was the second slug that killed him. Instantly, straight through the heart. Soundlessly, the outlaw's legs buckled as a stream of red spurted fountain-like from his punctured chest.

Before the lifeless cadaver had crumpled to the ground, Carver swung the heavy Dragoon towards Kid Silvers. But the desperado possessed the innate split-second reflexes of youth. Both guns spoke as one, the thunderous roar echoing across the sandy wasteland. Black powder smoke billowed around the four protagonists creating an almost ethereal montage.

'Double-crossing skunk!' The Kid's blisteringly hate-filled expletive punched through the opaque void. 'I should have done for you back in Redemption and dumped yer miserable carcass alongside that other turkey.'

The swirling tendrils of smoke were rapidly dispersing, egged on by a stiff wind that had suddenly blown up.

Peg-Leg Carver lay on the ground, unmoving.

Neither Link Taggart nor his recalcitrant brother had been idle during those few fleeting moments. It was Marcy Waggoner who had been stunned into frozen immobility by the violent affray. And Kid Silvers had taken full advantage of her bewilderment.

Grabbing her round the throat, he was now using her as a human shield, his revolver jammed into her ear.

Link had dived behind the bulky torso of Patch Montana, gratefully palming the outlaw's fallen handgun. He gave thanks that the guy was built like the proverbial brick privy, affording him a half-decent place of concealment, provided of course that he kept his head down.

Separated by a ten-yard expanse of level sandy ground, they were in what could only be described as a Mexican stand-off.

But each knew that it could only be temporary. Something would have to give.

Silvers arrowed a cold look of scorn towards the bundle of rags that had been his ex-partner in crime.

'That old bastard got exactly what he deserved,' he hollered, tapping the cold steel of the revolver against Marcy's trembling cheek. 'Nobody pulls the plug on Kid Silvers and lives to tell the tale.' He spat viciously at the bleeding wreck. 'Now it's just you and me, eh Link?'

'It doesn't have to be like this, Corby.'

'You're right there, brother.' Silvers began edging towards the horses, using the girl as a shield. 'I aim to ride out of here with the girl. And there ain't a damn thing you can do about it. That is if'n you want to save her pretty hide.' He let fly a couple of shots, the lead slugs thudding into Link's bizarre haven. The dead body of Patch Montana shuddered under the impact, blood seeping from the punctures. The Kid gave a mirthless chuckle. 'Just so's you know I mean business.'

Link chewed dirt. He had no chance of returning fire for fear of hitting Marcy.

'You harm a hair on her head,' he ranted, 'And I'll hunt you down—'

'You ain't goin' no place, brother,' the Kid butted in, spitting out a stream of rabid curses. 'I'm takin' the broncs with me. You might have scuppered my chances of strikin' it rich, but there's no way I'm about to shake hands with the Devil just yet awhile.'

Link was stymied. Stuck betwixt a rock and a hard place.

That was when he noticed a movement to his left.

It was the old prospector. He was still alive, and with the Dragoon in his hand. But how would that help turn the tables on Corby. He had to do something, and fast. The Kid was already close to the horses.

Then he had it.

A gun duel! Appeal to Corby's overbearing arrogance. Link knew that he was no match for his brother when it came to the fast draw. Would Corby's need to prove his superiority outweigh his desire to split the breeze?

There was only one way to find out.

'How about we settle this business once and for all,' he

155

called. 'Man to man, just the two of us.'

Corby's mouth puckered in a surly pout.

'A gunfight. You and me alone. Winner takes all.' Link tried to keep the tension from his voice. This had to sound convincing.

The Kid scowled. An impatient shrug indicated his low opinion of the idea. 'Why should I risk my life when I can ride out of here?' he jeered.

Link's response was coolly threatening, delivered in a flat monotone devoid of emotion or sentiment. He laid a caustic eye on his brother.

'Because if you leave me here, you'll always be looking over your shoulder, wondering. Jumping at every shadow. Studying every face. And one day, I'll be there. By then you'll be a nervous wreck and death will come as a blissful release.'

A silence followed.

Kid Silvers knew his brother. Link would never give up until his own particular brand of justice had been administered in full. He also knew that he could take his elder brother left-handed if necessary. Link could handle a gun, but he was no gunfighter.

'Straight down the line?' Silvers called back. 'No tricks?'

'Straight as a billiard-cue. Everything on the level.'

A pregnant silence ensued while the Kid weighed up his options.

'OK, it's a deal,' he said. 'We leather our weapons and step out into the open together.'

'You got it, Corby.'

The Kid growled.

'And don't call me that. The handle's Kid Silvers.' He coughed, hawking a glob of phlegm into the dust. 'That other jerk is dead and buried.' Then he uttered a manic cackle. 'Just like you will be in the next couple of minutes.'

The brutal termination threatening this man whom she had come to admire was too much for Marcy. Tears welled up in her eyes. Too late she realized that there was more than just mere affection plucking at her heart strings.

'Don't do it, Link,' she cried in desperation. 'He'll kill you.'

'Sorry, Marcy,' he murmured. 'But this is the way it has to be. Things have gone too far down the line for it to be settled any other way.'

'The girl can flip a coin,' suggested Silvers, flexing the fingers of his right hand. 'When it hits dirt, make your play. And may the best man win.' He offered his brother an oily smile as he hunkered down into the classic gunhawk's stance. 'Ready when you are, Link.'

There was one final task that Link needed to perform to ensure that things worked out as he fervently prayed they would.

'Move over here, Marcy.' He indicated for the girl to shift over to his right. Then he remarked, for his brother's benefit: 'Just so's you're out the line of fire.'

'Now!' hissed Silvers.

Marcy whimpered. Her whole body was shaking uncontrollably.

'Do it!' snapped the Kid, spearing her with a scornful glare. Link gave a tight nod of concurrence.

The two men faced one another, each holding the other's gaze. Waiting. Watching as the silver dollar spun high into the air. The gyrating metal winked and sparkled in the clear light, circling in parabola flight, a messenger of fate. Achieving its zenith, the only way forward was down, down, down.

The two men tensed, nerves strung taut as a drumhead. Fingers hooked clawlike above the butts of their revolvers.

Three seconds. Two. The coin was inches above the sandy floor when gunfire erupted from an unexpected quarter. Silvers clutched at his belly as blood poured from the fatal wound. It was a gut shot, not a killing hit but sufficient to stop the guy in his tracks.

The Kid's mouth hung open registering total surprise at this abrupt change of fortune. Swaying, trying desperately to stay on his feet, his watery gaze shifted to the right from where the shot had come.

'You . . . still . . . alive . . . old man?'

The choking retch was instantly cut off by a second blast from the Dragoon. It punched the Kid back to the rim of the mesa, where he teetered precariously before disappearing over the edge of the abyss. A blood-curdling shriek, cold and unreal, animalistic in its intensity, ripped through the heavy atmosphere.

Link sank to his knees, head bowed, shoulders slumped. His breathing was ragged, blood pounded in his head. He felt no sense of satisfaction. There was no joy in having just been the cause his brother's demise.

Marcy rushed across, cradling his distraught face in her hands.

'It's all over, Link,' she cried tearfully. 'You weren't to blame. Corby had gone way past the point of no return.'

Then Link remembered his saviour.

Struggling to his feet, he lurched across to the old-timer. But the effort of turning the tables on his one-time partner had been too much for Peg-Leg Carver. He had paid the ultimate price. Yet rather than a pained grimace cloaking the gnarled contours, he appeared to exude an aura of serene composure, as if well-satisfied with the outcome. There was even the sly hint of smile on his lined face.

And as for the hidden gold-strike, its elusive location lay at the bottom of an inaccessible ravine. And as far as Link was concerned, that was the best place for it.

Death in all its brutal guises had stalked the high country of Clark's Fork. Three men were dead, and Link had survived only through the valiant sacrifice of an old prospector down on his luck.

When he got back to Moose Jaw, he would ensure that both the old guy and Beartooth Crockett would received the finest of funerals. Their names would be carved in stone. Legends of the frontier, synonymous with all that was courageous and inspiring to future generations of settlers.

Three weeks later Link Taggart returned at last to Cimarron, and a father anxious to learn the whereabouts of his missing son. Link had dispatched the briefest of wires from Denver to give warning of his imminent return. It contained no details. The old man deserved the truth face to face.

So when only a single rider hove out of the early mist surrounding the Box T ranch buildings, Jacob couldn't help but fear the worst.

Link had ridden all through the night on the final section of the long trip back from Wyoming. He was caked in yellow dust, his deep-set eyes bloodshot and weary. This was a reunion he had played over in his mind a hundred times. What was he going to tell his father?

Drawing Smudger to a halt outside the ranch house, he dismounted, slapping the loose dust from trail-soiled clothes. A dozen ranch hands ceased their morning chores, angling curious peepers towards the newcomer. They were all eager for news of their missing *compadres*.

Not until he was inside the house did Link utter a word. Jacob Taggart held his peace with difficulty until the grim story emerged in all its finality.

Though, in the telling, reality was shelved in favour of a more acceptable version in deference to Jacob's feelings. No father wants to learn that his son has turned into a vicious, cold-blooded killer.

Spike Nolan became the villain of the piece, Corby the one who had sacrificed his own life to save that of his elder brother.

Jacob Taggart accepted the story at face value. It was what he wanted to believe. If he suspected the truth, he gave no hint. Displaying an outwardly proud bearing, he stared out of the large picture window, any hurt effectively buried beneath the bluff exterior.

'Soon as I've settled matters over here,' Link finished, pausing to sink his third glass of lemonade, 'I'm heading back to the Yellowstone.'

The ghost of a slow smile traced a pattern across the sweat-stained visage smoothing out the tense strain that had built up over recent weeks. He felt that a huge weight had been lifted from his shoulders. Marcy Waggoner had promised to help him resurrect Beartooth Creek. And, who knew, maybe after a while she would join him up there on a more permanent footing. His final comment was casually delivered in a low murmur.

'Got me some unfinished business up that way.'